What the critics are saying:

Ms. Lapthorne did something unusual with the werewolf genre. She made a true love story with no violence, no dark corners, and no deep seeded anguish. This story was beautiful in the fact that it was emotionally poignant..... It was a perfect balance of eroticism and romance. I personally cannot wait to read more of the Rutledge Werewolves! HIGHLY RECOMMENDED - *Sara Sawyer,– The Romance Studio*

The werewolf genre is one of my favorites and this book lives up to all of my expectations. It is full of emotional drama and tension that kept me interested all the way through. - *Angel Brewer, JERR Reviews*

I liked this story because it started off different from all the other stories where the heroine is pregnant. Usually it builds up to the point where she becomes pregnant, but when this story starts she already is expecting. I definitely liked Sophie's character, as well as the fact that Artemais had brothers. That always adds a better swing to the story. And it also opens up many possibilities to the brothers having their own stories. Besides that, I loved how Aretmais's brothers played the part of Sophie's friendship circle. They were the ones who knocked some sense into Aretmais. Priceless! - *Kelly, Sizzling Romances*

SCENT OF PASSION
An Ellora's Cave Publication, September 2004

Ellora's Cave Publishing, Inc.
PO Box 787
Hudson, OH 44236-0787

ISBN #1-4199-5045-2

ISBN MS Reader (LIT) ISBN # 1-84360-869-3
Other available formats (no ISBNs are assigned):
Adobe (PDF), Rocketbook (RB), Mobipocket (PRC) & HTML

Edited by *Martha Punches*
Cover art by *Syneca*

SCENT OF PASSION:
RUTLEDGE WEREWOLVES

Elizabeth Lapthorne

This series was a huge undertaking for me, and couldn't have been completed without my very best friends. So I dedicate this in particular to old friends: Danni, Mar, Martha and my sugar daddy as well as my new friend – Peggy. You're the very best of friends a girl could hope for and I love you all totally.

Chapter One

Sophie looked down at the innocuous blue line and for the first time in her twenty-seven years of life felt frozen with shock. After staring numbly at the line for a moment, she snapped back to reality and reached for the box. Checking that the strip in her hand really did match the picture on the back of the box, she swallowed and tried not to panic.

Damn, blue really does mean positive.

Fearing the whole situation was some sort of cosmic joke, with shaking hands Sophie hastily used the second test from the box.

If these damn things didn't make mistakes, there's no way they'd give out two in a packet, right? Must be something faulty with that test, she silently assured herself, as she calmed down.

Blue again. *Well, hell. Twice in a row. I wonder if I need another box? There's just gotta be a chance this box was screwed up in the factory.*

Sophie wondered at the odds of this pregnancy. Almost six weeks ago, on the winter solstice, she had thrown caution to the wind. Leaving all the papers and files she had brought home to read and review, she left her work behind in her little one-bedroom apartment. She had dressed herself up and, determined to give herself a much needed break, had gone down to the local bar and partied all night.

After a few glasses of wine, followed by a vodka—or two—she could feel the beat and pulse of the music sing through her veins. There was a live band playing and the drum seemed to call to her, beckon her almost. The deep, steady beat pulsed through her like another heartbeat calling out to her own. Silently admitting to being slightly tipsy, she had leapt up onto the stage and started dancing around the band of edible looking men.

Not being a consummate partier, she wasn't surprised she didn't recognize the band. After being so wrapped up in her work for the last few years, she had lost touch with the local bands trying to make it big. The more she drank and danced, the more she mourned the lost wild woman that dwelled, deeply hidden, somewhere inside her.

The Howlers were four drop-dead gorgeous men, all buffed up with varying lengths of dark brown hair and sexy bedroom blue eyes. Even in her slightly tipsy—or more-than-slightly-tipsy—mood Sophie had felt an electric and instant attraction for the drummer.

The singer was tall and lanky, with a voice that could easily woo and cajole each and every woman in the bar to do indescribable acts. The sax player looked to be the youngest of the brood, and had been winking at a number of the younger girls screaming out for him on the edges of the packed dance floor. The bass guitarist had the longest hair, falling in waves halfway down his back, and even though she hadn't seen him grin like the other two, he was still a damn fine specimen of sexy male, a make-your-panties-wet fantasy man.

But there just seemed to be something about the drummer that caught and held her attention.

Usually she felt attracted to the powerful business-man-in-a-suit style; but this drummer was every woman's secret fantasy. The dark and dangerous bad boy.

The drummer had the shortest hair of the lot, being cropped fairly close to his head, but something about the way he held himself back; his almost, but not quite under control demeanor, told her *he* was the one in charge of the small and surprisingly good band.

Dressed in a suit he could have walked into any boardroom and easily commanded the attention of every person present from the top manager to the lowliest secretary.

He had a presence. Power appeared to simply cling to his large frame and ooze out of his pores.

Sophie had danced until the very early hours of the morning when the band had finally finished up. When the drummer offered to buy her a drink, then led her off to a dark corner of the now packed bar, she hadn't resisted in the slightest. It had been a short jump from there to following the sexy man home.

Sophie knew her inner wild woman was awakening. The sexy voice and intense way this man made her feel was more than enough reason for her to follow him back to his apartment. Promising herself this one night of passion and indescribable sex, Sophie felt no reservations at all.

Even though she hadn't been drunk by the time they had arrived at his small apartment—within walking distance from the busy bar—she had still been on a buzz from the alcohol, adrenaline from all the dancing, and pure excitement. It had been ages since a man had made her feel so excited. Her last lover had left her more than four months ago, stating he simply couldn't be with someone who could only organize her social life around work and what currently resided in the "today" section, under Personal Appointment Calendar on her PDA

Sophie had tried to explain that her diary and calendar helped her organize everything simply so that she wouldn't forget an important event, but Steven hadn't been listening or interested by then. Sophie knew her greatest fault was that she tended to forget anything not written into her schedule or tattooed on her forehead.

Yet she doubted she would ever forget the drummer.

Artemais.

Even now, she smiled as she recalled their conversation on the slow walk back to his apartment. When he had initially introduced himself, she had wondered briefly if it was a stage name, to make him sound more exotic.

Yet when she had asked for his real name he had smiled wryly and explained that Artemais *was* his real name.

She had laughed, and demanded his explanation of such an unusual name. With a laugh and a sexy glimmer in his eye, he had pronounced his name very slowly, *Art-eh-MAY-is*. When she repeated it after him like a dutiful child, he had laughed, taken her hand and continued their walk.

He explained back when he had been born, the family name of Artemis — the God of the Moon — was supposed to be bestowed on him. Yet in the two days previous to his birth, no less than three other mothers had provided their children with the then-popular name.

According to his grandfather, his parents had been undaunted by the sudden popularity of their chosen first-born's name and had spent the remaining forty-eight hours and then the full eight hours of labor "discussing" alternate names to their originally chosen one.

Extremely surprised to find such a fairly normal explanation to such an unusual name, she had asked him to finish the story. Even in her sobering-up state, she knew her curiosity had gotten the better of her, but there was also the way she felt captivated by the soothing cadence of his voice. She knew she could happily sit and listen to him talk to her forever.

Artemais chuckled and snapped her attention back to their conversation. Sophie felt slightly silly at her naïve, romantic thoughts. Artemais continued, explaining that as his head had crested his mother's womb, she had screamed and declared "Artemais" was close enough, and damned if she would have an unnamed firstborn while they continued to try and compromise.

Entranced by the birth of his firstborn and new son, Artemais' father had capitulated and the matter was over.

Thus, he had been named.

Sophie laughed and declared though his name was truly exotic, it did seem to suit such a gorgeous man who drummed so well. As they continued their leisurely walk, Sophie learnt that the other men in the band were his younger brothers, and she smiled thinking about the resemblance between the men.

Artemais certainly to her was the most delicious of them, but one could never account for personal tastes. Not that it mattered—none of the four sexy men had lacked for willing women throwing themselves at them that night.

Spending the next six hours having mind-blowing sex with Artemais had Sophie nearly incoherent with lust and satisfaction. All thoughts of work and her lonely state of life had abated in the sheer force of their lusts and sheer volume of mutual orgasms.

Sophie performed acts she had only fantasized about previously, truly letting out her inner wild woman in every sense and wallowing in the pleasure and gratification that came from their acts.

Grateful she had woken up first the following morning, Sophie mentally debated for five minutes what to do.

Morning-afters and relationship questions were not her forte. Yet she felt kind of sneaky simply dressing and casually leaving.

She dithered, very unlike her usual self, about whether to raise the question of his sexual health. The last time before she had collapsed into sleep, overcome with lust and passion in that moment, she had completely forgotten to place a condom on Artemais.

As she used the pill, it seemed easy enough to squash her pregnancy worries. Surely one night didn't matter?

A few days later, Sophie noticed she had missed a day's pill. Again she brushed the thoughts aside—the chances of her getting pregnant were still slim to none. She would be fine.

When her period hadn't arrived on time, she hadn't been too worried. Off the pill, she had been the most irregular woman alive. Pre-pill as a teenager, anything from three to eleven weeks had been common to her barely pubescent body. But it was now nearly nine weeks since her last period and she was fretting.

Now here she was, with only one sexual encounter in nearly six months, *two* positive pregnancy tests and one skipped period. She was probably six weeks pregnant to a man she had only met once, and had dreamed about almost nightly since.

You dreamed of the sex, she reminded herself, *not the man*.

Sophie felt her legs wobble when she thought of the erotic, almost pornographic dreams she entertained in her mind nightly since her time with Artemais. It felt as if her dream body sought him out and seduced him over and over—or maybe his dream self sought her out for seduction.

Either way, every single night over the last six weeks she had entertained fantasies so explicit, so erotic, she became wet merely thinking of them. She couldn't even tell if half the positions they used were physically possible, so intricate and complex they were.

More worrying still were the tender aftermaths of these encounters. Artemais would hold her, cuddle her, stroke her short curly locks and murmur sweet nothings into her ear, telling her she was the only one for him. Worse was the way she would tenderly stroke his chest, his shoulders, cup his face and respond to these soft words of love, giving him her love in return.

Soon enough their small caresses and soothing, soft love words would turn steamy again, and their lusts would take over, but Sophie had come to crave her dreams for the soft, post-coital words of affection as much as the mind-blowing good sex.

Sophie tried not to think guiltily about the fact she now avoided the district of the small bar like the plague, even driving out of her way to avoid it. She didn't want to come across Artemais again and humiliate herself by drooling—or worse—casting herself at his feet and begging for another night of the better-than-fantastic sex they shared. She had finally managed to convince herself he didn't think of her at all, even if *she* dreamt of him nightly.

Just thinking about the dreams, even now, worried as she was, made her wet. Artemais—his dark blue eyes gleaming in the soft moonlight, his tanned chest beckoning to her hands and her mouth.

Her dreams had filled some secretly yearning spot inside her that she had never known lay empty. And now there appeared to be a baby.

Sophie felt her legs weaken again, and she sat on the rim of her tub.

It wasn't that she didn't want a baby. She hadn't planned on having one, and certainly not from a one-night stand, but now that she was pregnant there was no question about keeping it, and raising it happily and healthily. Her problems centered on her lack of relationship with the father.

What is the protocol here? she wondered. Did she contact Artemais? Would he expect it from her? Surely he deserved to be informed of her situation? She didn't need, nor want money from him, yet it seemed incredibly unfair not to inform him he would soon be a daddy. She didn't care if he didn't want anything to do with their baby, yet neither did she really want to raise a baby by herself.

Deciding to shelve her problems until the following morning, Sophie showered and got herself ready for bed. Making a mental note to book a doctor's appointment for a blood test the following morning, she quickly fell asleep.

Strangely, for the first night since the Solstice, her dreams that night were not the lusty, erotic dreams she was now used to. They were…strange. She seemed to be winding deeper and deeper into some sort of silky trap, a trap made of midnight blue and forest green.

The smell of damp earth and pale, silvery moonlight cast shadows over trees and outdoorsy kinds of places. A tiny baby with deep blue, achingly familiar bedroom eyes, and her own blonde curls lay wrapped in pure white linen, cradled protectively in her arms.

Gazing in awe at her little baby, Sophie realized with that instinctive knowledge that only came to her in dreams, that her little baby was a girl—and she was perfect.

Cradling the warm infant tenderly in her arms, Sophie looked around her. They were in a large forest, the dark brown earth damp and soft beneath her feet. The midnight blue sky illuminated by stars overhead. Giant, dark green, thick trees surrounded them, giving the whole scene an earthy, slightly surreal feeling.

The forest was a dark, dark green, that lush, inviting color only very old trees could give. The mixture of dark brown, dark green and midnight blue created a canvas around Sophie and her little baby girl.

She felt excited and safe, not fearful in the least, even though she had no idea where she was. For a moment, stupid as it later felt, she was certain Artemais was around somewhere close, watching her and their baby.

In the distance, wolves howled. Neither she, nor her perfect little girl was scared or worried.

Chapter Two

Artemais woke up with a huge, very smug, very satisfied masculine smile on his face.

He had *known* she was the One. He and his brothers had set up their playing in a local bar this time around. They had traveled all over Montana, searching futilely. When none of them had found their True Mates in the state, they had moved around to encompass the surrounding states, even as far west as Seattle.

Constantly looking, but never finding *her*.

Neither he nor his brothers had been totally certain how they would recognize their True Mate. It was one of the very few things the curious boys-becoming-men didn't have the heart to press their old Grandfather on.

The Old Man got tears in his eyes each and every time he reminisced about "His Naomi". Even now, twenty-five years after the massive culling that had killed his beloved wife, their only son and daughter-in-law, Zachariah Rutledge broke down in tears when thinking or talking about his lost True Mate.

As always, Artemais felt a small pang of sadness when he thought of his dead parents. When he was ten, and his brothers eight, six and four, their parents and grandmother were killed in the National Park. They still lived in the old estate, specifically built by his ancestors, backing onto Glacier National Park. Even though they had fought hard to keep their estate over the years, it was integral to their life, so during their moon time they could run free and wild as their wolf -selves.

But twenty-five years ago, unrest had crept up on many of the citizens surrounding the National Park. One man who, even now, no one really talked about had created a large stir. On the night of the full moon, many of the wolves, both natural and from the Pack were killed.

It was an old wives' tale that the wolves running in the forest would harm any human they happened along. Each and every werewolf in his pack knew the harsh penalties for even scaring, let alone harming a human.

Artemais—while his senses were totally different as a wolf—was perfectly cognizant of what he was doing while running in his wolf form. He was interested in the scents of the earth, in the pull of the moon, in the joy and rapture of the hunt—he didn't become some rabid beast out to drink blood and feast on human flesh.

While his sexual appetite might be huge, he had no desire to kill or maim anything other than possibly a wild rabbit if he had failed to eat earlier in the evening. The old horror movies showing hairy men turning into rabid wolf-beasts and eating virgins and munching on children was nothing more than an old boogeyman story.

Along with more than a dozen other wolves his parents and grandmother had been killed.

During the battle, Zachariah sustained a number of mortal wounds. Massive head and body wounds over long weeks and months healed into scars the Old Man still bore. The internal scar of losing his True Mate, however, had never fully healed. After all this time Artemais and his siblings worried that particular scar might never fully heal.

Six months after the attack, Zachariah returned back to their ancestral home, physically healed enough to take care of himself and watch over his four unruly grandsons.

Artemais knew the Old Man had done his best—raising the boys with a firm yet gentle hand. He listened to their worries, soothed their childhood fears and paid no heed to their pranks. In many, many ways the four brothers knew they owed their happy, carefree existence to the Old Man. They also owed their strength and full adjustment to what, for many others, would have been an inconsolable loss to him.

Yet the only help the Old Man had been able to give them were tear-filled memories he shared of the first meeting of His Naomi. The way he became enveloped in her scent, the way he hungered for her from the moment he saw her. Not just a physical connection, but to hear the Old Man talk, it was an emotional and almost psychic connection as well.

The Old Man, certainly no blushing romantic, had firmly described it as a soul-connection. Even all these years later, he insisted to each of his grandsons that they would know when they finally came across it. All four men had been disgruntled, having to accept the Old Man's word for it.

The only other advice Zachariah had passed on to the four young men had been that only one's True Mate could bear an Alpha's children. Thus the responsibility fell heavily on Artemais' shoulders to find his true mate and bear an heir. That way, not only would his brothers be able to roam further around and find their own mates, but the bloodline of his father—and the pack's true Alphas—would be secure.

At first, Artemais hadn't believed his grandfather

about his seed only being fertile to his True Mate. When he had fallen hard for his puppy love a number of years ago, he spent two fruitless years trying to get the woman to conceive.

Though Zachariah no longer permanently lived in the ancestral home now that the four siblings were fully grown men, but roamed the world for longer and longer periods of time, he constantly kept in email contact. Zachariah had gently suggested to his eldest grandson that he was being truthful about the fact an Alpha was infertile to any but his True Mate, and Artemais' desperation to impregnate his puppy love was futile.

Artemais had been polite to his grandfather, yet privately disbelieving. Yet as the frustrating months and years had passed, he finally accepted that only his True Mate could carry his seed. Anyone else was infertile to him.

Artemais also worried about this often on a different level. He had never fallen in love again—and he didn't like Fate playing with him like this. The realization that only one woman could carry his child, and thus only one woman could he mate with and be fertile with, shattered him. As master of his own destiny, he would have much preferred to choose his own mate.

Yet it was not to be.

As the years passed, each and every doomed encounter simply frustrated him more and more. His anger had grown, both at his position and at the intricacies of Fate. He hadn't truly understood how he would recognize his One, as woman after woman failed to bear his seed.

He was tired of traveling, tired of the constant,

emotionless fucking. He missed his big home, missed his huge forest and parklands, where he could take the form of his wolf without worrying about who would see him, and where he could roam free and wild.

It was an act of sheer homesickness and desperation, which had him convincing his brothers they would perform in one of the local bars. It had been over an hour's drive from their home, but they all had small apartments in the local city where they could rest overnight with their respective pick-ups.

And then he met Sophie.

The instant she had walked into the bar he could *smell* her. From all the way across the bar through all the smells of alcohol, smoke, lust and the dozens of other scents, he had scented her fresh flowers and light, mossy, wonderfully feminine smell.

When he finally got a good, clear view of her, he nearly dropped his drumsticks and rushed over to her, picked her up and mated with her there on the floor.

She seemed small to him, but then, at six foot one, many women were small to him. She might have been around five-five, five-six at the most. Curvy, but slim. Short blonde curls framed her expressive face.

Physically she was appealing, but it was her scent that drove him wild. He couldn't get enough of it, or of her.

As she had danced around him and his brothers, he had constantly closed his eyes to draw her scent deeper into his body, his cock hardening. He had tried to hide both his cock's reaction, and his own desperation to scent her fully, to draw her close and explore every part of her body with all of his senses. She intrigued and, unlike any other woman of his acquaintance, drew him on levels he had never experienced before, from the short curls on her head down to the fire engine red polish on her toes.

Desperate and half-wild with lust at the richness of her flowery scent, he had been extremely afraid she would spook.

Never had retaining his control, both of his beast and of his sexual lusts, been such a problem. His brothers had ribbed him mercilessly the following morning when they had woken him up from the deepest, most satisfying sleep he had had in years.

When he realized she had left him, he had gone wild with worry and frustration. His brothers' playful teasing had brought his mind back to reality, and he started praying she had fallen pregnant.

He searched his mind for every tiny scrap of information, every name she had dropped with her tongue loosened by the alcohol. Piecing together every moment they had spent helped ease his ache, his worry. Harassing Samuel, his private eye brother, and shamelessly utilizing every record his security company could access, within a matter of days he had a wealth of information on his Sophie, including her home address.

After those first few days had passed, the waiting set in. He had sent an email to his grandfather—but for the life of him he couldn't recall what he had said. Last night he had received a reply, warning him that his Grandfather was heading back home, although he had no idea of his return time.

Artemais prayed constantly that Sophie had conceived, that she was the one whom he could spend the rest of his life adoring and loving.

Staying away from her had been a torturous hell, but

there was no point in allowing himself to continue a relationship that was sterile when he was supposed to be moving heaven and earth to find his True Mate. Even if the woman in question made his mouth water at the mere memory of her body and scent.

The waiting nearly killed him. So he had invaded her dreams and her fantasies, determined to have as much of her as possible until he knew for certain, until *she* knew if she was pregnant or not. She would soon know that True Mates knew just about everything about each other, even the small, intimate details.

And last night he had found out. She was his.

She had become pregnant with his baby — undoubtedly a boy child, as all his traceable family and ancestors were male and probably always would be — but nevertheless, it was *his* baby.

Spending every night with her in her slumber, he knew the baby was his. She'd had no carnal relations other than the fantasies and dreams he shared with her, nor had a baby been growing inside her womb when he had spent the night wallowing in her body and scent.

But she was damnably human, and now he had to work out how to woo her without scaring the pants off her and having her run away.

He would think of something, he always did.

Jumping out of bed and hastily dressing in jeans and a shirt, Artemais made a mental list of things to take care of before he went into the city. Debating the wisdom of telling his brothers about his pregnant almost-mate, he figured not telling them would create more trouble than telling them would.

It was his turn to wake up his siblings, and what a

proud moment it felt for him. Knocking on each of their doors, he thanked the heavens that all his siblings were home last night. This was not something he would be allowed to live down if it occurred over the phone.

Telling each of his brothers to meet him down in the kitchen in ten minutes, he returned to his room to pack a small overnight bag. Still uncertain as to how he would convince Sophie to come back here with him, he realized he might need to spend the night with her to help convince her.

He knew that his life would never be the same, and yet he couldn't help but be glad for it. No more hunting for his Mate, no more feeling alone. Now there would be a woman in residence, hopefully, year round. Someone important for him to come home to. Someone for him to love and be loved by in return.

Frowning, he realized just how big a change this would make in both his own life and Sophie's. It truly hit him just how large a change he was asking of her. For perhaps the first time he really considered how hard it might be to convince his True Mate to leave aside her own life and come join his. The more he thought about the changes he was asking and expecting, the more serious his mood became.

Resisting the impulse to pack any toys, he shoved a clean shirt, socks and pair of briefs into the small bag along with his wallet.

Determined to try and put a positive slant on his suddenly somber thoughts, Artemais grabbed the keys to his Jeep, and hefted his bag over his shoulder. He left his bedroom, eager to start the rest of his life.

Bouncing down the stairs, bag slung casually over his

shoulder, Artemais came through into the kitchen and beamed at his disgruntled and tousled-looking brothers. Opening the fridge and nabbing an apple for breakfast, he slammed the door shut and faced his family.

"I'm going to be a daddy," he announced. Instantly the three grumpy brothers turned into excited, eager uncles.

"Really? Who is it?"

"It was that chick from the bar, right?"

"When do we get to meet her?"

"Have you checked out her background?"

"You lucky devil you."

"Does she have a sister?"

"Does she know what she's getting herself in for?"

"Has she been to a doctor yet?"

The last comment, from William, had everyone sober up a little. Artemais wasn't going to admit to his brothers that he had invaded Sophie's dreams each and every night since they first slept together and he hadn't been physically in contact with her since that night.

"No, but she's planning to go sometime today. I'm driving down and will meet up with her tonight. I just wanted to tell you all before I left."

"I'll come with you. No knowing what mess you'll make of trying to bring a human out here. They're not all those pliable, brainless bimbos you've been searching amongst, brother dear." William insisted.

Dominic laughed.

"Oh, and *you* have so very much experience with the headstrong type? You've been grumpy as hell now that you've finally met a woman you can't seem to charm and wrap around your little finger, not that you let us meet her. *I* have the most experience with charming the woman here, so I think I'll come along and make sure you don't dig yourself deeper into the hole you're already in."

Before Artemais could issue a scathing retort at his two brothers, Samuel cleared his throat and jumped in.

"Actually, I was planning to go into the city for a few days to...er...do some research. So there's no need to waste all that gas. Might as well come along with you three."

Artemais raised an eyebrow, doubting the legitimacy of Samuel's work, but realizing none of his brothers were going to miss this golden opportunity to make him writhe in embarrassment. Sighing, he nodded. When Dominic slapped his back and jeered, Artemais struggled not to grin.

"Cheer up, old man. If your lovely mate decides to make life hard for you, we can always come to your rescue. Tell her a few stories about your wild single days and how *The Howlers* is such a huge joke. You know I'm always happy to step up to the plate for you, if you don't feel you can rise up to the challenge."

Artemais growled and grabbed his youngest brother by the throat. Jerking him up against his body, he simmered down as Dominic laughed out loud. Realizing he had been baited, he let his brother go and gruffly ordered, "I'm leaving in ten minutes, with or without you all."

The hasty exodus and slamming doors showed that at least his brothers believed some of what he said. Artemais closed his eyes and wrestled his temper back under control. Picturing Sophie, all spread out before him, golden curls gleaming, pale thighs spread, picked his pulse up for a totally different reason.

Only partially aware of his three brothers filing past him out to where the large Jeep was parked, he took a deep breath, ended his wicked fantasy of eating Sophie, and locked the door behind him.

Time to go hunt his mate.

As he climbed into the Jeep, his brothers rowdily jeered and complemented him on his prowess. As they started singing one of their favorite bawdy songs about this woman from East Tipples, with the large, incredibly luscious nipples, Artemais finally relaxed and allowed himself a huge, toothy grin.

Chapter Three

Sophie parked her little Suzuki in her apartment's underground car park and rested her head wearily on her steering wheel.

It had been worse than the day from Hell.

An average day in her job as a Personal Assistant to the manager, or Personal Slave as she liked to think of herself, for the godson of the CEO of an advertising company could easily be described as a day from Hell.

Not only were average duties such as making coffee, typing reports, organizing calendars, taking dictation, and keeping the office running smoothly part of her job. But other extras that particularly annoyed her were instances when her boss brainstormed ideas with her when "he wanted a woman's point of view". *She* knew he used her ideas and carried them out as his own—but proving such was almost impossible.

Sophie had found herself fantasizing more and more frequently about simply not turning up one morning and telling her boss where he could go shove his male chauvinism and abuse of power.

Yet she had been making progress with the top managers. They had begun to notice all her work and effort, and a few quiet noises had been made of them opening a new position for her. So she had been patient and put up with the chauvinistic comments, pats on the ass, and sly winks.

Until this morning.

This morning, she had carelessly asked one of the other personal assistants if she had known how long the company's paid maternity leave was. She had been incredibly unlucky in that her boss had been entering the room right at that moment, and obviously overheard her remark.

Twenty minutes later he called her into his office. She knew from the smug grin on his face that soon everyone from the CEO to the janitors would know she was pregnant. Her visions of a bright new start in a higher job blew up into a puff of smoke.

She exploded when her boss had made a smart remark about her finally realizing her place in the world. She had uttered a few very unladylike remarks about her boss's parentage, upbringing, outlook on life, and his life expectancy. She quit on the spot.

Ten minutes later she had collected her meager belongings, typed up a resignation—which she had been mentally writing for months, anyway—and left the building without a backward glance.

All thoughts of making her doctor's appointment forgotten, she had spent the afternoon indulging herself by eating Ben and Jerry's to celebrate her newly unemployed state.

Sophie had no idea where she would go from here, but her resume looked very healthy, and her background was flexible and adaptable. She was a natural organizer and shouldn't have too much trouble picking up something temporary while she thought about the future.

She visited the library to scour the reference section and borrowed everything they had on pregnancy and prenatal care. A brief flip through the introductions of a few of the books showed her one of the most important and commonly overlooked aspects of prenatal care was a healthy diet.

A vision of her practically bare fridge and cupboards flashed through her mind. She smiled at the thought of the ice cream nuggets and vintage cheese and crackers she had been planning on consuming for dinner. Packing up her bags and borrowing the library books, Sophie headed off for a quick stop by the supermarket on her way back home. At the checkout she made a mental note to remember to pick up tomorrow morning's newspaper, to search through the employment section. She also made a note to search online later tonight.

Reminded of her mental "to do" list, Sophie lifted her head from the steering wheel, picked up her satchel, heavy due to all the books crammed in it, and her two bags of groceries. She locked the car and headed towards the elevator.

Pushing the call button, she tapped her foot, impatiently waiting for the car to arrive. Usually she climbed the three flights of stairs to her apartment for the exercise, but today she simply couldn't be bothered. With the strain of her day and the heavy satchel of books and groceries, Sophie forgave herself the soft treatment.

As the elevator took off, her stomach rolled uneasily. Thinking she should have missed that second serving of Ben and Jerry's, she hoped she wasn't coming down with a bug.

As the elevator lurched, arriving at her floor, Sophie realized her stomach was having a serious turf war over something. Stepping gingerly out of the car, wondering what the hell was going on in her stomach, she realized with a startling clarity that she was going to be sick all over the hallway.

Running flat out to her door, she stuck the keys into the lock and rushed inside. Dropping her satchel and groceries carelessly onto chairs and tables, she ran into the bathroom, and just barely made it to the toilet.

A minute later, she sat weakly onto the floor, removed her shoes and contemplated the wisdom of standing back up again. *Who ever heard of afternoon sickness?* Sophie smiled wryly.

"Here," a deep, recognizably sexy voice drawled. "This might make you feel a bit better."

Even as her brain recognized and registered Artemais' sexy voice, she shrieked and jumped up onto her feet. Feeling instantly dizzy and worrying that she was going to lose whatever was left in her stomach, Sophie teetered for a moment before a big, warm hand clasped her around the arm, steadying her.

"Wipe your face, Sophie. Are you sure you don't need to…er…go again?"

Face flaming in embarrassment, Sophie took the wet washcloth from Artemais' other hand and buried her face into its cool depths. Taking a deep, soothing breath to gather her nerves, Sophie lifted her head again.

"What the hell are you doing in my apartment? And how did you find me? And why *now*?"

When Artemais merely smiled that devastatingly sexy smile of his, Sophie groaned and put her face back into the washcloth.

"You left the door open in your rush to enter the apartment. It took me a while to track you down, but I finally found you from another guy in the bar. I've been searching for a while."

Which was true, Artemais consoled himself—he'd been searching for her since his eighteenth birthday. It mightn't be exactly what she would assume his words to mean, but they were truthful nevertheless.

Sophie took careful, deep breaths, inhaling the fresh, warm scent of her washcloth. Today certainly wasn't turning out how she had anticipated.

She had mentally rehearsed how she would tell him about her pregnancy a number of times throughout the day. Yet she always managed to push it back out of her mind.

Before she could manage to arrange her thoughts, he solved the problem himself. Gesturing vaguely out into the hallway where she had dumped her bag and groceries, with a casual ease she envied, he commented, "That's an interesting book collection Sophie. There something you want to tell me?"

Uncertainty and panic entered her brain. Her body, still shaking from the rather brutal expunging of her ice cream, left her gaping like a fish out of water. Feeling her stomach roil, whether in fear or sickness she couldn't tell, she turned back to the toilet, retching miserably.

A pair of strong, well-remembered hands held her gently, and began to wipe her forehead soothingly as she emptied the last of her stomach's contents down the toilet.

Yeah, one hell of a day, her brain remarked.

Chapter Four

Artemais held Sophie very gently, half-afraid she would break. He had never been attached to a pregnant woman before, he wondered if morning sickness was usually so severe. *Or afternoon sickness for that matter*, he silently laughed. As Sophie finally quieted down, he helped her stand, and led her to the basin to wash her face and brush her teeth.

Holding her so close, he couldn't help but be drowned in her scent. That light, flowery, slightly mossy scent that now would always indicate freedom and passion to him. Her scent drove him wild, made him hard and nearly brought him to his knees. Her scent would always make him feel and remember their burning passion.

Desperately trying to focus his thoughts, he reminded himself that his woman was sick and feeling weak. Jumping her bones and wallowing in her scent was not a good idea. Worry slowly crept into his brain. Was it safe for a pregnant woman to be sick like this?

"Uh, Sophie, are you sure you don't have a tummy bug? Should I pack you off to a doctor or something?"

Barely even looking at him, she shook her head and continued cleaning her teeth. She didn't appear worried, but Artemais was concerned now. When she finished rinsing her mouth, he pressed her.

"You sure?"

Sophie sighed.

"Look, I was just fine 'til I got into that elevator. It's always been pretty jerky and unstable, it simply upset my stomach. That's all, I'm just fine."

Artemais looked closely at her, she looked so pale, so weak. Her short curly blonde hair shone, but her face seemed pale, her gray eyes were a little wary.

"Maybe just to be sure..." he started, but Sophie exploded, cutting him off.

"Look macho man, I was just fine until you and your...bunch of Howlers turned up at that damned bar. Now, thanks to you, I have no job and get to look forwards to three to six months of *afternoon* sickness. I've been looking after myself for a number of years and will probably manage to scrape through a pregnancy just fine. Please don't let the door slam you on your way out."

Artemais grinned. He loved a feisty woman and much preferred this Sophie to the pale and washed out one he had been speaking to a moment earlier.

As Sophie pushed her way past him out of the bathroom, he watched her sweet ass sway. Even angry as she was, he felt his gaze heat up as she bent down to pick up the spilled satchel of books, giving him a perfect view of that rounded ass he had loved so much that one night.

He couldn't wait for her to settle down into his house. She was certainly feisty enough to fit in with his rowdy brothers. They all lived together for the most part in the main house, but with separate entrances and lots of room, there was more than enough privacy when needed.

As she picked up her satchel and glared at him, commenting, "Well?" He couldn't help the grin from spreading on his face. She had obviously realized he was staring at her ass.

"Well, what?" he countered. "You have no job, I have a big house. Why don't you come with me while we work out what you want to do?"

Artemais blinked at the shocked expression on her face. *Not the most tactful of invitations*, his brain mocked. Maybe Dominic was right, maybe he did need his brothers here to help smooth the way a little. They were across the street, probably pacing in the park.

"Are you out of your mind? I have known you for less than forty-eight hours. I have a decent amount in my savings account, I'm sure I'll manage. I don't need to be a kept woman, thanks all the same."

Artemais winced, *Damn, where are those brothers when I need them?*

"I didn't mean to suggest... Look, I just want a part of raising my son. Surely you can't begrudge me that?"

And in the meanwhile I can woo you and keep you close, his brain interjected.

Sophie raised an eyebrow mockingly, almost as if she heard the ending his brain tagged on. Instead, she surprised him yet again, picking out the smallest of his comments.

"Son? Who said this child would be a boy? It could just as easily be a girl, you know."

Artemais shrugged. *He* knew it would be a boy; all the children in his lineage were boys, so would this one be, but there was no reason to shatter her illusions.

"Sure, but I'm warning you, all the children on my side of the family tree have been boys for generations. But that's beside the point. I want you to come live with me, so we can talk about the future. If you're determined to stay here I can crash on the couch or something." Artemais indicated his backpack.

"No way am I simply moving in with you. You could be an axe murderer for all I know."

Artemais grinned a big, toothy grin. He wasn't an axe murderer, but he could tell they both still had surprises in store for each other.

"I'm not an axe murderer. You saw no bloodied axe in my apartment, did you?"

Artemais enjoyed the blush that spread across her face at his reference to their night of passion.

"Well, no…"

Artemais cut in on her blushing, stammering response.

"And we already have a little boy growing inside you. I think that lends us a certain level of trust, don't you?"

Sophie glared at him, refusing to back down.

"I'm not letting you carry me off, he-man style."

Artemais watched her looking around the small apartment rooms, and he crossed his hands over his chest, letting his body language show he wouldn't leave without a fight.

He felt his worry lighten as she sighed and stared back up at the implacable expression on his face. He grinned at the grudging, decidedly unfeminine way she gave in, totally without grace.

"I guess you can crash here for a night or two while we talk over matters. I suppose there are some things we need to discuss, like Lamaze classes, names for the baby, and living arrangements. But one wrong move from you, buddy, and you can go back to your own apartment and we can meet in restaurants to chat. Agreed?"

Artemais looked at the firm set of her mouth and jaw. Much as he wanted to lean forward and caress and kiss the stubborn tilt, he knew when to quit his pushing.

"Deal. But if I start to cross the line, you're to warn me. This is a two-way street here, I'll try and be accommodating, but I have the feeling we're going to butt heads on certain issues, so no letting me cross the line then tossing me out without a fair warning, okay?"

He felt a thousand times better as Sophie's face lit up with a grin. At least they had reached a point where they were both happy, if only for different reasons. Sophie casually bent over and started picking up her satchel of books.

"Deal. Can you cook?"

Artemais smiled.

"Sure can. But can I introduce you to my brothers first? They're across the road and simply dying to meet you."

Sophie narrowed her eyes and paused in her gathering of the books. She looked him over slowly, and he wondered what it was she was searching for.

"I don't mind taking a brief walk over to the park. Then we can come back here and you can cook us up some dinner. As I'm sure you would have noticed, I've been shopping and am exhausted." She nodded over to the grocery bags lying discarded on the coffee table. "Sound okay?"

Artemais swallowed. He certainly hadn't gotten everything he wanted—but this wasn't a perfect world. Sophie was prepared to let him stay with her, so he had a shot at convincing her he wanted the whole deal, her, their baby, and a life together, always.

He nodded his head in compliance.

"Sure thing. I can put away what you have as well. Between those groceries and anything I can scavenge around your cupboards when we get back, I'm sure I can whip us up something light for dinner. I don't want to make anything too heavy that will make you feel any sicker."

Sophie looked at him once more with that strange look in her eyes. He wished he could tell what she was thinking.

"Artemais, are you sure you want to do this? I swear I'll keep you in the loop with everything. You really don't need to—"

Artemais angrily cut her short.

"Yes, Sophie. I do need to do this. I'm sorry it took so long to get in touch with you. It's a bit complicated. Look, I want to be here, I want to be a part of your life. Of *our baby's* life. I want to be here—or I'd have merely called you or left a message somewhere. Let's go meet my brothers before we start our first argument, hmm?"

Sophie searched his face again, obviously noting his determination. Picking up her coat from where she dropped it on the floor in her haste to get to the bathroom, she grabbed her keys and headed towards the door.

Praying for strength and help, Artemais followed the woman he was determined to make his mate, shutting the door firmly behind them.

Chapter Five

Sophie huddled in her coat as the chilly Montana wind tried to push her about. She muttered mentally to herself, determined not to cave in to Artemais like some brainless, helpless female. She had no desire at all to raise her baby alone. She was firmly of the opinion that if at all possible children needed a mother and father. Yet neither would she grovel and blindly follow a man she barely knew.

She wasn't convinced meeting Artemais' brothers would help her determination to stand firm, yet these men obviously meant a lot to him. If she had close family around, she would also want to introduce Artemais to them.

A part of her still reeled from the whole encounter with Artemais in her bathroom. *He wants me to live with him, make us a family*, she kept reminding herself. Everything seemed to be happening all at once. Forty-eight hours ago she had been working hard to make her way up the corporate ladder. Now, she was jobless and six weeks pregnant, agreeing to let a man she barely knew live with her for an indeterminate period of time.

Shaking her head, she wondered if she would wake up soon and laugh herself silly over her strange dream.

Sophie mentally went over a list of her objectives. Lists always seemed to help her.

Top of that list was getting to know Artemais better.

She didn't need to make a decision right away, but she needed to know the father of her baby better before she made any conclusions about their future.

When Sophie realized her paces were almost double-time, practically running to keep up with Artemais fast, long-legged pace, she slowed right down to her normal stride.

"Could you please remember not all of us have six feet of legs? I am not meeting your brothers after running to catch up with you and sweating like a pig after a marathon race!"

Artemais stopped and to her total surprise, blushed. Sophie caught her breath and stared. He looked adorable with the faint pink tinge across his cheeks. Thankfully, he slowed his pace right down to match her more sedate steps.

"Sorry," he grimaced, "I was just thinking of all the catastrophes my brothers might have started in the half hour since I left them."

Sophie blinked. The three men she vaguely recalled from that drunken night at the bar had been stunningly gorgeous, yes, but not so stunning that she would think that women would lay down at their feet in the middle of a public park!

Yet as they came closer to the gazebo in the middle of the park, she could make out three tall, dark-haired men, with two women who had evidently stopped jogging to chat to them. One seemed to be playing with some sort of micro-sized PDA, another had his hands in his pockets studiously ignoring the two women's giggling overtures. But the third one had an arm around each lady and was evidently enjoying himself immensely.

"Dominic," Artemais growled under his breath, surprising her, "I swear I'm going to have to chain that wolf down one of these days."

Artemais caught himself as Sophie looked at him, an eyebrow raised in query.

"Uh…Dominic is a bit of a ladies' man, a wolf on the prowl. You know?"

Sophie confused by the half-baked explanation, but too intent on watching the three men they were heading towards, let it slide.

Dominic had been the saxophone player and looked to be the youngest of the brothers. With shoulder-length hair the same dark brown of his siblings and the same dark blue eyes, he could certainly pass as sex personified. At around six foot one, and with his largely muscled body, she could well understand how he and his two brothers could have grabbed the ladies' attention long enough to deter them from their afternoon jog.

The men, hearing their arrival, stopped their chatting and turned to watch her. Feeling slightly embarrassed, Sophie blushed and slowed her steps.

"They won't bite," Artemais assured her, "they're just curious."

Raising her eyebrow at him, determinedly pretending she hadn't been concerned in the least Sophie tilted her chin. By meeting his brothers she was simply being polite, it didn't signify anything permanent—no matter what Artemais thought.

Dominic finally noticed their arrival and withdrew his arms from around the two ladies. Pulling a scrap of paper from his wallet, and scrounging a pen from the brooding brother, and got the ladies' phone numbers. The two women hastily scribbled, then waved as they resumed their running. Sophie felt a twinge of nerves as three pairs of hot blue eyes turned to face her.

As she and Artemais came to a stop, Dominic smiled and leaned forwards. Brushing a chaste kiss to her cheek, he grinned.

"Welcome to the family. I take it you're Sophie, the mother-to-be?"

Sophie felt her eyes widen in shock. *How the hell had he known?*

"How...?" she tried in vain to politely phrase her question.

Dominic merely grinned hugely.

"Women have been badgering us for years about how they have an instinctual knowledge, yet you think men can't have instincts too?"

Sophie couldn't help herself. She simply had to smile back at that contagious grin and zest for life.

"Mmm...maybe. Are you telling me you have women's intuition?"

Dominic laughed. He was masculine on so very many levels it simply wasn't possible for his ego to be dented by the slight jab.

"I have masculine intuition. I just *know* things about ladies. Don't I, Artemais?"

When Artemais merely rolled his eyes and his other brothers made various gagging motions, Sophie laughed even harder, accepting that this man would definitely *know* certain things about the ladies.

"You must be Dominic, then, the soon-to-be chained down youngest brother."

"Oh-ho! Brother dear can try," Dominic laughed at Artemais, "but think of how cruel it would be to disappoint all those lovely ladies!"

Artemais merely shook his head.

"Sophie, meet Samuel and William, my other two brothers."

Sophie grinned as Samuel put his PDA into his pocket, and leaned forward to kiss her.

"Pleased to meet you. Where's your luggage?"

Sophie laughed.

"Sorry to disappoint you guys—but I'm not coming back with you. Tempting though the offer is, I'm not the sort of girl who moves in with four strange men whom she's known for less than a few days."

Three sets of eyebrows rose, and Sophie could swear she felt Artemais squirm next to her. Suddenly, both Samuel and Dominic bent over laughing hysterically.

Sophie turned to William.

"Did I say something funny?"

This merely made both Samuel and Dominic laugh even harder, as William tried to explain.

"Artemais has practically raised us from pups—kids. He has this way of making us do what he wants us to without raising his voice or forcing us to. He simply makes it close to impossible to do anything *but* what he wants. Let him hang around for a while—you'll understand soon enough."

Sophie raised an eyebrow. Living by herself a number of years had made her fairly set in her ways. She had a sinking sensation they might be butting heads in the very near future.

Samuel finally righted himself enough to gasp out, "To think! Artemais and his legendary appeal—" Sophie raised an eyebrow in query as Samuel began choking on his laughter. *His legendary appeal?* her mind wondered. Before she could question his half-finished sentence, Dominic tried to talk through his tears of laughter.

"His famous address! Gone the first time he finds a woman he truly wants! It's...it's...just too funny for words!"

Artemais, simmering next to her, finally gave up.

"Oh shut up you two. This is not helpful."

Sophie looked at William and caught his eye. He too had seen the laughter glinting in their blue depths, but he restrained himself much better than his younger two brothers. "You will have to excuse my younger brothers. They are at the ripe, mature ages of thirty-one and twenty-nine. Still babes in the wood, as I'm sure you understand."

The undercut scored its mark, and both brothers regained control over their fits of laughter.

"I'm sorry, Soph," Dominic started, only to be interrupted by Samuel.

"Yes, honestly, it's just so funny to see someone actually stand up to Artemais and not be cut down in seconds."

"We stand behind you one hundred percent. Seriously. Give him hell."

Sophie chuckled at Dominic's attitude.

"Well, I'm sorry, but I have no intention of giving him hell. We're merely going to talk about the arrangements for the baby and sort out what we'll do."

William raised his eyebrow, but couldn't get a word

in edgewise as both Samuel and Dominic were determined to speak their piece.

"Well—surely you will eventually cave in and come out to live with us. There's plenty of room, we rarely trample all over each other. And the boy needs his space to grow and become wild and free."

"Truly, we won't stomp all over the new love nest," Samuel added, "the house is quite private when one wants it to be. And the backyard goes straight out into the forest, so there's more than enough play area for the little guy."

Sophie felt touched at their pleas, but quite unmoved from her determination.

"I truly appreciate what you guys are saying—but I'm quite happy here in the city. I have my own little apartment, and I have no intention of holding my *child* for ransom. You are all more than welcome to come visit at any time, I have a very comfortable couch, as Artemais is about to learn."

Sophie tried hard not to grin at the snickers and furtive looks all his brothers shot Artemais. He sighed stoically and tried not to rise to their bait. He simply raised an eyebrow in a manner that could only be called lordly and gave her a *look*. She had a sinking sensation that this man had no intention whatsoever of sleeping on her couch.

*An argument for a different time, Soph...*she reminded herself.

"Anyway," she continued, determined, "the baby and I will certainly come out to visit you as often as possible."

Deciding the time for a change in the topic was called for, Sophie looked at each brother in turn, finishing with William.

"What's with this certainty everyone has that the child is a boy? Haven't you heard genetics gives a 50/50 shot at gender being a boy *or* a girl."

William stepped forward, a mere breath away from her. Sophie wasn't very intimidated, William didn't emit any scary sort of vibes, but she certainly felt a little confused, having no idea what his intentions were. William placed a large hand over her stomach, pressing very gently.

A little shocked by the intimate gesture, her eyes flew to Artemais. He merely smiled and nodded, obviously knowing what his brother seemed to be doing. Sophie, still unsure, tried to move infinitesimally away from the large man, but he held his other hand to her back. He in no way hurt her, he simply held her still and seemed to study inside her stomach, as if he could see or contact the tiny baby inside her.

He seemed so somber and serious when compared to his feckless, carefree brothers; she hadn't the heart to kick up a stink just yet. When he leaned closer to her, hand still gently but firmly pressed into her still-flat stomach, Sophie bent her head up, expecting him to kiss her cheek in welcome, as both Samuel and Dominic had. When William merely inhaled her scent, she was perplexed and getting a little scared.

He moved back, but kept his hands resting where they were.

"She definitely carries your child, Art," he said in his quiet voice.

Sophie took a step back, and William allowed his hands to fall back from her stomach and back. She wanted to question...to protest the strange actions, but before she could articulate any sound, Samuel and Dominic were whooping with delight and clapping Artemais on the back.

She felt herself being lifted off the ground by William and swirled around in a circle. For the first time, she actually saw him smile—a huge, gorgeously brilliant smile that lit up his face and features. The man was totally beautiful when he smiled, and could easily rival his brothers with the ladies. After only seeing him somber and serious it came as a total shock to realize he was just as handsome, if not more so than his two younger brothers.

For just a second, she idly wondered what made this man seem so somber. A split second later she realized trying to answer that question might integrate her with this family more. By trying to help them and learn more about their personal situations would make it even harder for her to stay strong and learn about Artemais and his family before committing to something permanent with them.

As the knowledge registered in her brain, she decided to not question and pry. The thought of helping William, of trying to solve whatever dilemma dogged him persisted, but Sophie firmly squashed her instinct to try and help this man. His smile was truly beautiful, and for now, his being happy with her and Artemais' baby was enough.

Thank heavens he doesn't smile that often, she thought, *or else women everywhere would get a bad name for casting themselves at his feet constantly!*

"Well done old man," Dominic teased Artemais, "Another fine addition to be brought into the Rutledge family. Just think, another little boy to join the pack."

Pack? Sophie's brain stirred, reminded by the wolf comment, but instantly discarded it. *Just odd wording*, she assured herself.

What grabbed her attention was the single-minded knowledge with which these men instantly assumed her child was going to be a boy. Sophie intuitively knew there and then that she would have to fight for every scrap of independence in this family, with these four overbearing men, she would certainly have some interesting conversations.

But she would never be alone again, her mind consoled her. She knew without a doubt that even if things didn't work out between her and Artemais, she and her child would always be welcome with these men.

"Who said this child would be a boy? I don't see any ultrasound photos? *I* think this child will be a girl, and she's going to kick *all* your asses." *Or wrap us all around her little finger…*her brain mused as she smiled.

As William set her down gently on the grass, she felt the four brothers circle her, dwarfing her. All except William smiled smugly, assuring her that it *might* be a girl in that pompous tone she was coming to know from Artemais.

Despite their lectures on the apparent male-only offspring ratio of their heritage, Sophie politely ignored them all, focusing on William. He remained silent, and she raised an eyebrow at him. He appeared to think for a moment, then shook his head and kept his own council.

Finally growing weary of the lectures, she interrupted them all, mid-sentence.

"I'm hungry. Artemais is cooking me dinner. You're all so big my apartment might get a little cramped—but you're all welcome to come and join us if you're not fussy and promise to help with the dishes."

Sophie looked around at the four men still circling her. Unbeknownst to her, Artemais glared ferociously at each of his brothers, over her head, so she didn't notice.

William was the first to draw her into a huge hug.

"That's okay, little sister. We need to be heading on back, anyway. But thank you very much for the invitation. Please come out to the big house soon, and we can all show off our expertise on the grill. If you're expecting Artemais to cook for you you'll soon be craving some *real* food anyway."

As soon as William released her, Dominic picked her up in a huge bear hug. Feeling like a kid again, her feet dangling a short way above the ground, Sophie squirmed.

"Dom! Please put me down, I'm too heavy to lift like this!"

Dominic laughed, but did place her back on her feet, though he kept her wrapped in his big hug.

"Seriously, Soph, Artemais' cooking is like old Dickens food. Gruel, porridge…"

"Watery stew, with barely any meat or vegetables in it…" came Samuel from behind her. Dominic moved back with a wicked grin on his face and Sophie turned to hug Samuel goodbye.

When she finally pulled back, Artemais came up beside her possessively and linked his arm through hers.

"That's enough you guys," he growled, not quite angry, but getting there. "If you scare off my…woman, I'll slaughter the lot of you."

Sophie frowned, a bit concerned, but all three brothers

laughed and slapped him on the back in a friendly manner. None of them paid the slightest heed to his threat, and very soon Artemais was also laughing and joking with them, his anger completely evaporated.

Sophie grinned as she realized Artemais had only been semi-serious in his threat, and by totally ignoring it, his brothers had shown what a load of rubbish it had been.

Artemais led her to a Jeep, left by the side of the road on the other side of the large park. The brothers shook hands with Artemais, which Sophie thought manly, but odd, and each gave her a last kiss goodbye as they climbed in to the Jeep.

Waving them off, Sophie and Artemais turned, arms still linked, to head back to her apartment.

Sophie frowned when she realized she didn't think of her apartment as home, but merely as her apartment.

Thankfully, the comfortable silence between her and Artemais continued down the street, and she pondered her thoughts. She didn't really have a place she called "home", like Artemais and his brothers called their big house "home". She resisted the impulse to lay a hand on her still-flat stomach.

The temptation to go back to Artemais' place, his home, was strong. Yet her mind couldn't reconcile following a strange man, even one whom she had slept with and now bore his child, when she had known him for less than a few days.

Sophie made up her mind. She would get to know Artemais better, both for her own sake and for that of their unborn child. Once she knew him better she would reassess her options and move on from there.

Chapter Six

Artemais finished preparing the two salads and the dressing while he waited for the pasta sauce to simmer. The water for the pasta finally began to boil. Now he had to wait for the sauce to finish simmering and then he could cook the pasta. He smiled to himself at his thoughts. Everything checked from his mental checklist, he let himself relax. Everything was under control for dinner.

He could still hear water running in the bathroom, so he knew Sophie hadn't yet finished her shower. Either she was avoiding him, or she liked to indulge herself with long hot showers.

The thoughts that arose from helping her get clean in a long, hot shower had his cock rock-hard again, and him nearly panting with desire. Keeping his hands off her would certainly prove difficult, if not impossible.

Steeling his mind away from his lascivious thoughts, he started cleaning up the kitchen. As he always cleaned as he went while cooking—it was an easy task to tidy the last few items up, and very soon the running water penetrated his brain again.

With the way things were shaping up, he'd be pouncing on Sophie the instant she walked out of the room. Her scent inundated the tiny apartment, saturating the chairs, the air, every item in her small apartment. He felt her presence here as strongly as if she were standing right behind him, waiting to grab his ass or hips and turn him around.

His boner so hard he feared he'd split the seams in his jeans, Artemais desperately tried to adjust his pants for a more comfortable fit. With the size his cock was, he knew restraint would be an exercise in futility, but anything was better than thinking of Sophie. Sophie, naked and wet in the shower, waiting for him to come and scrub her back, nibble her shoulder playfully, soap her lovely body into creamy anticipation for him to ram his hardness...

Pushing himself away from the bench he leaned against, Artemais paced the small room like the caged beast he was quickly becoming.

With the scent of his passionate Sophie surrounding him, coaxing him, daring him, he felt every breath threaten to push him beyond his limits. He desperately wished for Sophie's erotic scent to fill his own rooms in the main house, wanted to feel her body over his, and have her scent all over his possessions, have her small knickknacks and books next to his own.

He wanted them to be a family, he realized. Not merely for his son's sake, but because he had never felt this intensity for another woman. Never wanted to wallow in her body, in her laughter and passion.

Fearing that her scent would truly start to make him lose his mind and control, he stalked out of the kitchen, preparing to pace the rest of the apartment.

As he entered the main living room, his eye fell on the dropped satchel of books Sophie had left in her rush to enter the bathroom earlier that evening. Happy to find a mess that needed clearing, he bent to pick up the satchel and place it more neatly on the table.

Grunting, he hefted the surprisingly heavy satchel. Since when did a few romance novels weigh so much?

Not feeling the slightest twinge of worry, he was merely satisfying his curiosity of the borrowed books, nothing else, he opened the unlatched satchel.

Inside were more than a dozen books, all crammed haphazardly into the large satchel. Glancing at the titles, Artemais felt his curiosity peak even higher. *101 Things to Know About Pregnancy; The First Trimester — What to Expect; Doing it Alone — The Modern Woman's Guide to Raising a Healthy Baby Alone; Pregnancy: The Herbal Way, How to Safely Eat, Drink and Have Sex Without Hurting Your Baby.*

Artemais stopped at this title. *Eat, drink and have sex* rolled around in his brain, taunting him and flashing all manner of erotic and highly explicit pictures in his mind. He might have only physically had sex with her for one night, but the last six weeks of their dream loving hadn't satisfied him fully, it merely whetted his appetite for more. Researching and finding the safest and best way to bring his Sophie pleasure without harming their son suddenly became his first priority.

Carrying the book back with him into the kitchen, he stirred the sauce, pleased to see it coming along, but it definitely needed at least another ten minutes work.

For the first time Artemais noticed the shower had been turned off. He now could hear Sophie opening and closing drawers. Resting one hip against the sink, so he could read and keep an eye on the sauce simultaneously, he opened the book.

Completely forgetting the satchel sitting on the table, Artemais flipped to the contents page. Quickly finding the chapter about the information he desired, he flipped to that section of the book.

Stage 1 — the first trimester months: the book started. *As long as your wife/partner is feeling okay with the idea, it is more than safe to still have sex…*

Engrossed, he started to read.

* * * * *

Sophie ran a comb through her damp curls. Warm and satisfied from her shower, now casually dressed in a pair of baggy tracksuit pants and an old sweatshirt, she was at her most comfortable.

During her long, luxurious shower she had debated mentally at length. At no stage since learning of her pregnancy had she thought to exclude Artemais from their baby's life, yet neither did she find herself fully prepared to blithely go and live with him as if they had always planned it thus.

Frowning slightly at her reflection, she tried to sort out her thoughts.

She couldn't deny her attraction to Artemais, she craved his touch and his body. Yet this was lust speaking, passion, not a lasting commitment, which living with him would entail.

Sophie took a deep breath and returned the comb to its spot on her dresser.

She was starting to fret. Maybe she needed food to calm her mind, her thoughts always ran away from themselves when she got hungry.

She opened her bedroom door and the delicious smell of carbonara sauce wafted in from the kitchen. Glancing at the pile of empty and half-empty packets neatly stacked on the bench, she noticed that Artemais cooked traditionally enough that he used Italian bacon, pancetta, and not normal bacon rashers.

Sophie smiled whimsically, a man who could cook, and cook very well from the smell of the simmering sauce, was a treasure worth hording. Her mouth watering at the scrumptious scent of freshly cooked pasta, she pushed the softer feelings aside until only the scent of the creamy white sauce and cooking bacon resided in her mind. Through the open doorway she could see Artemais leaning against the window casually, reading one of her books.

Deciding not to interrupt his reading, she refrained from calling out to him and simply crossed the room. As she walked across the room, she finally registered the title of the book he was reading.

Embarrassment made her face flame a dark red, outrage welled in her chest.

How dare he go through her satchel!

Opening her mouth to yell at him, she nearly snatched the book from his grasp, when she remembered her hasty entry into the apartment earlier that evening. Mentally picturing herself dropping her satchel with no thought to where it lay, her outrage dimmed slightly.

He hadn't been snooping, probably just picking up after her. *But even so*, her inner demon insisted, *why is he reading this particular book?*

Sophie sighed. Despite herself, and knowing full well she wasn't the sort of girl to usually indulge in casual sex, she had been curious to learn what would and wouldn't be safe sexually for her baby. With her erotic dreams becoming more vivid over time, instead of less vivid, she knew that sooner or later she would have tracked

Artemais down. Once they were in the same space, she had known sparks would fly, and the possibility of sex became almost a given.

"I take it you're not looking up what foods are best to eat while I'm pregnant?" she finally conceded. There was no point in getting upset that he was reading the book, when she, herself, had planned on reading it later that evening, before her world had been turned upside down with Artemais showing up.

Artemais looked up, grinned that cheeky, mischievous grin he did that made her melt each and every time she saw it, then went back to the book.

Shaking her head, unsure whether to laugh at him or hit him, she gently pushed past him to stir the sauce. Inhaling the rich, creamy fragrance with something akin to awe, she smiled despite herself. She would owe Artemais an apology for her remarks about his lack of cooking skills. If the sauce tasted even half as good as it smelt, he could definitely cook.

Just as she pondered whether to remove the boiling pasta from the stove, she felt Artemais' large presence behind her. He placed the book on the table and made a shooing motion.

"Back, woman! I'm the uninvited guest here, I'll finish the meal. How about you set up two places for us?"

As Sophie set out the places, she watched Artemais drain the pasta, place it next to the salads he had prepared and dribble the carbonara sauce over the pasta. Within minutes they were both seated and digging in to the delicious meal.

"I'm sorry I implied you couldn't cook. I definitely stand corrected."

Sophie felt her stomach roll with desire as Artemais paused in his eating. Looking her up and down, his eyes seemed to brand every inch of her flesh. There was a hungry, wicked glint in his eye that spoke of untold nights of ecstasy and a deep, lasting possession.

"I'm good at a number of things we have yet to explore. Goddess willing, we'll have the time and opportunity to...explore them together."

Sophie steeled herself not to shudder in reaction. She well remembered that deep, husky quality to his voice, and what it symbolized. On that unforgettable night, the deeper into his lust and passion they both fell, the huskier his voice became. It were as if all his energy and blood centered and became controlled around his groin and in his passionate lovemaking. Everything else started to shut down, so they had been both too weak to walk, to speak coherently, to do anything except have mind-blowing sex.

Sophie determinedly shoveled another mouthful of the pasta into her mouth, so he wouldn't catch her drooling. Chewing far more forcefully than necessary, she concentrated on not stripping there and then and begging him to take her. She instinctively knew if she gave in to him physically, he would expect her to pack her belongings and move in with him. If she capitulated even an inch, he would take that and move in a mile.

Carefully sipping her water, she finally managed to get herself under control. Not wanting Artemais to know the direction her lascivious thoughts had taken, she decided it was time to change the topic of conversation.

"So what do you do when you aren't playing the drums in bars and having masses of women throwing themselves at your feet in ecstasy?"

By the wild, masculine grin that spread across his face, she knew he understood the direction her thoughts had taken. He knew exactly how deeply he affected her.

Bully for him, she thought. *He can just bloody well wait for me to get to know him better.*

As Artemais began to explain about the security company he owned and ran with the help of his brothers, the bulk of their conversation through dinner stayed well away from babies, pregnancy, moving and sex.

Sophie diligently ignored the many double entendres Artemais innocently managed to inject into their conversation as the evening progressed.

For his part, he ignored the small smiles and answering flames these risqué comments brought to her eyes on occasion. He was, thankfully, gentleman enough to not bring up either of their reactions to each other. Life felt complicated enough for her at the moment, so she was grateful for his gentlemanly behavior.

Around midnight, she felt her eyes begin to droop. Moving to the linen closet as she finished telling him about her day from hell and subsequent quitting of her job, she pulled down a number of spare blankets and a comforter from the cupboard.

"I hesitate to ask this sweetheart, but what are the blankets for?"

Sophie smiled tiredly.

"For you to make your bed out of, *sweetheart*. That is a perfectly fine couch you're sitting on. I've fallen asleep on it more than once over the years. It'll do just fine as a surrogate bed for you."

Sophie felt her gut clench as he simply shook his head.

"Maybe it's comfortable for *you* to sleep on, but I'm a

good six inches taller than you, and no way will my frame fit comfortably on that!"

Sophie looked from his tall, looming figure and back to the couch. She realized that it would be too short for him, and though a part of her rebelled not to care, the softer, more caring side of her knew she wouldn't insist he sleep on it.

"Well then, I suppose I could —"

Artemais interrupted her before she could even finish the thought.

"Do not even suggest it. It's far too cold here at night for you to even consider sleeping out here. I give you my word of honor I won't ravish you in the middle of the night. I simply want to have a comfortable place to sleep."

Sophie looked from Artemais to the couch. She trusted his word of honor. Over the last few hours, they had talked at length on every topic imaginable. He made her laugh and made her ponder different trains of thoughts. He certainly seemed to be a decent, honorable man, and her instincts were rarely wrong about people.

"You *swear* you won't touch me?" It wasn't really him she was afraid of; she felt far more wary of herself and her own reactions. Sophie wasn't certain spending the night sleeping half-naked next to this man was the soundest idea she ever entertained. She knew she felt fiercely attracted to him, and she knew from the glint in his eye he also had quite an attraction to her. If she could get his promise not to touch her, then it would help steel herself to not pounce upon him the second they came next to each other in her big bed.

"I have no doubt we will touch each other, but I swear not to initiate any sexual contact tonight. That is as good as

I can do, love."

Sophie and Artemais looked carefully at each other. Sophie knew this was her chance to prove to herself, and him, that she could deny her physical passions and keep herself in check.

"Okay," she sighed, "let me get changed. You *do* have something decent to sleep in — don't you?"

Artemais waved to his small backpack, sitting on the floor by the couch. He grinned wickedly.

"But of course."

Sophie sighed again and went to her bedroom. She had a feeling the night was only beginning.

Chapter Seven

Artemais squelched the urge to fidget. The bedside clock Sophie had read 3:04 am, and he had a raging hard-on that refused to budge.

Sophie lay next to him, curled up against his body like a small kitten. All she needed to finish the image was a deep, throaty purr of satisfaction. She lay pressed ankle to head cuddling into his warmth, and it was slowly driving him mad. Every now and then she would murmur and rub against him, as if seeking a way to get even closer into him. Her legs shuffled restlessly, entwined between his own larger, thicker legs. Her arms circled his waist just below his ribs, mere inches above his iron-hard erection.

After the first hour he had given up trying to keep her at arms' length. Resigned, he stretched one arm out to hold her closer to his body in a more comfortable position for them both. The warmth of his body, or maybe just the fact that she now felt comforted and held, settled her enough that she could sleep deeply, totally unaware of the slow torture she put him through.

Artemais looked down at his woman. The pale, thin moonlight that wasn't filtered through the midnight blue curtains was enough light for his wolf eyes to see the perfection of her skin. If anything his mind had dulled his memories of her perfect skin, satin soft and her pale blonde curls.

Self-preservation, obviously, he grimaced.

The thought of having to lie chastely next to Sophie for even a week's worth of nights was enough for him to moan in despair. His cock, hard and randy, primed to explode, ached and made him inch ever closer into madness. He dare not even touch himself for relief, for fear he *would* explode everywhere—and explaining to Sophie why he had jacked off in her bed was not a conversation he wished to hold. Everything about this woman drove him wild, to the very brink of his sanity.

Her soft curls. Her small sighs of sleepy happiness. The way she nuzzled the juncture between his neck and shoulder. The way she entwined her legs around his, as if she were a vine trying to climb him.

More distracting than all of these was that light, mossy scent that permeated his thoughts and would likely haunt his dreams for all eternity. With Sophie draped half over him, her scent transferred itself all over his skin. She, her happiness and her scent, penetrated his cells and into his very soul.

Everything combined to make him want to howl his frustrations to the nearly full moon, and take her over and over until he satisfied himself.

Yet underlying this driving need he felt to stake his claim on her were softer, more reserved feelings. He had always thought because Fate would choose his mate, they would simply breed together. He would never be unfaithful—it was not in him to be with more than one woman—yet never had he expected to have these strange feelings, feelings of protectiveness, possessiveness. He wanted to curl himself around his little Sophie and shield her from all the world's evil and harm.

She tugged on his heartstrings, he realized. She made him want to stroke and soothe her, give her the moon and stars.

Artemais gently touched her silky curls. The short blonde curls reminded him of golden sunshine and sweet honey. Framing her face, one minute they lent her the air of a mischievous imp, yet in the space of a heartbeat they made her appear hot and sultry and the sexiest seductress he had ever encountered. She was a complex conundrum and he looked forward to getting to know her better.

Unfortunately he needed to be back at his ancestral home within the week. The night of the full moon drew closer, and he would need the night to run free and wild, but also to help hunt with his pack, to lead them, as his duty dictated, and as he had known all his life.

Artemais continued to stroke Sophie's hair as he thought. He had just under a week. A week wherein he needed to show her how she loved him, addict her to his taste, admit to her that he was a werewolf and their son would be the next pack leader. On top of that, he needed them married before the baby was born — to secure any breach of technicalities in the future.

Great. No sweat.

Artemais had confidence in himself, yet even he, in this dark hour of the night, worried it might be too much, even for him. He knew he couldn't make Sophie love him. He continued stroking her soft curls, thinking and thinking.

Refusing to become melancholy, he smiled as his natural optimism kicked in. They already had this strange bond he could not explain or describe. This electric feeling between them made him care about her, more than just the incredible fucking they shared. As he felt this strongly about their bond, it made a lot of sense that she felt the same for him.

Artemais pondered his strange thoughts as he stroked Sophie's hair. True to his word, he kept his touch light and gentle. In no way did he attempt to wake her up with his sensuality. Sidetracked from his more melancholy thoughts, he began to fantasize about what to show her and do with her when he took her back home with him.

Groaning, he realized he had come full circle in his thoughts, back to his iron-hard cock. Giving in to his lust, he continued to fantasize, keeping his touch on Sophie light and gentle. More of a caress to soothe himself.

A short time later, she stirred in his arms. Worried she would cry foul of his gentleman's promise he instantly stilled his hand. The soothing gesture had been giving him a sense of peace, but he didn't want to argue with her over his honest intentions.

Sophie only partially woke up, murmuring something he could not catch.

"I'm sorry, sweetheart, I didn't hear you."

When Sophie buried her head further into the warmth of his neck, pulling him even closer into her embrace, he replaced his arm around her shoulders, drawing her nearer to his body.

The tiny straps of her green camisole had fallen down her shoulders hours ago, but her matching green flannel pajama pants still covered her decently—not that it hampered his memory or imagination any.

"I'm glad you're here. You won't leave me again. Will you, Artemais? I'm so tired of being alone," she sleepily murmured.

In that moment, Artemais knew she was still asleep for all intents and purposes. No way would she reveal this more insecure side of herself while cognizant.

"No love. I won't be leaving you, or the baby. We're going to be a family."

"Oh good," she responded, instantly falling back into her deep, regular breaths of sleep.

Artemais pulled her closer. Even though his cock was still granite hard, as it had been since the instant he crawled into her bed, he felt more at ease. More at peace. *I'm falling in love with her*, he dimly thought. He lusted after her fiercely, but these softer feelings, these feelings of protectiveness and possessiveness might just be the beginning stages of love.

Artemais meant what he had said. He would not be leaving Sophie, nor their child. He wanted a huge part in raising their son. That was part of it. But as they had talked into the night he had found himself enchanted by Sophie and her laughter, her sense of humor, in her insistence that she would always be fine and her optimism that everything always would work for the best.

She had overcome a lot by herself and always felt up to the task of taking on more. She was strong, self-reliant and brave, definitely a most worthy mate for him.

Yet nestled amongst all those other feelings lay the desire to keep that smile on her face, on keeping her happy, safe view of the world protected. And overriding all of these feeling sat his immense desire for her body, to wallow in her scent and plunge himself balls-deep in her over and over again.

If Sophie wasn't fighting him in her subconscious then half the battle was won. She might be stubborn and he knew she would fight him, fight their electric attraction while awake. But some deep, hidden part of her desired to trust him and follow him, wanted to cling and stay with him.

For now, it was enough.

Artemais settled back against the pillows, resigned to getting little sleep. He plotted his strategy for ensnaring his mate. His confidence fully restored with those sleepy, subconscious words from his True Mate, Artemais felt back in control and much, much happier.

Chapter Eight

Sophie woke up to the smell of bacon, sausage, and eggs cooking. She could hear Artemais whistling merrily in her kitchen, the radio tuned to some truly awful-sounding country and western music. Some man crooned on about love found but lost and a woman who betrayed him and broke his poor, aching heart.

For a moment, Sophie buried her head in the pillows, determined to ignore the large, sexy beast who threatened to take over her life. Her long-held independence quickly shot through her system.

Artemais was simply a man. A drop-dead gorgeous man, who made her pulse pound and the blood rush through her system, but still merely a man. She had learned a lot about him the previous night, his likes and dislikes, his deep and abiding love for his brothers and his absolute concrete certainty that they should raise their child together.

Even so, Sophie didn't believe *his* certainty to be enough to base a life together on.

People have made much more from far less, her inner demon taunted.

The tempting thought of following him back to his house, seeing how he normally lived hung before her, all shiny and bright. Squelching the dream, Sophie took a few deep, even breaths. It was far too early in the morning to contemplate such things. Easier for her if she simply took the day one step at a time.

And that first step would have to be out of this bed and into some real clothes. She wasn't sure she would be able to resist the reaction if she went out into the kitchen to greet her guest first thing in the morning only in her pajamas.

* * * * *

Artemais whistled happily to the twangy tune of the country western music station he had tuned into. He could never bear to hear people chattering to each other first thing in the morning, only to be interrupted once every fifteen minutes by a song.

He enjoyed the mornings, the fresh, cool air, the scent of the rising morning sun in the dewy breeze. Mornings always gave him a healthy appetite, and by the amount of pasta and salad Sophie had put away the previous night, he felt more than willing to bet his mate had a decent appetite on her as well, and would be equally hungry when she finally roused.

Just as the kettle boiled, and he pulled the last of the eggs from the skillet, he heard the bedroom door creak open.

Sophie came out in jeans and bare feet, a well-worn t-shirt completing her outfit. With her curls wildly ruffled, she looked adorable, as if she had merely run her hands through them.

She looked so sexy and so edible he held himself still as if she were the prey and he the predator. The urge to rush over to her, drag her into his arms and kiss her wildly, hungrily was nearly overpowering.

Artemais swallowed.

Firmly.

Discreetly clearing his throat, he pondered briefly which morning pleasantry to begin with, when Sophie beat him to the punch.

"Do you always listen to country and western music, or do you only torture everyone like this in the mornings?"

Perplexed, his brow furrowed.

"Pardon?"

"It's so damn depressing for first thing in the morning. Anyone would think listening to it that there wasn't a woman alive who could be faithful and true. If those bacon and eggs didn't smell so divine I'd have to pull rank and state `my house, my rules', but lucky for you I'm too starved to bitch about your taste in music."

Artemais grinned. Apparently his Sophie felt a tad grumpy first thing in the mornings.

"The music didn't wake you up, did it?" he asked, concerned, as he poured her orange juice.

He tried desperately not to chuckle as he saw her looking at the pot of coffee so covetously she fairly turned green from envy.

"No," she grumped, "but I would *really* appreciate some food. The baby is definitely hungry, she must have eaten all my spare supplies overnight. And what baby wants, she'd better get."

"Ah!" he exclaimed, serving her up a full plate of bacon, potato bites, eggs and sausages, "Now *that* is a Rutledge manly trait appearing. Our son is already proving his superior genes."

Sophie glared at him and bit down vengefully on the tip of the sausage. Artemais tried not to wince, but knew he had failed when he saw the glint of laughter in the gray eyes sparkling across the table at him.

Between the two of them, they managed to eat everything he cooked up, as well as drink down half a quart of juice. After listening to her bemoan for five minutes straight her unwillingness to drink coffee, for fear of the caffeine hurting the baby, he knew he also would be abstaining from drinking coffee in the mornings until her pregnancy finished. As she was a self-confessed morning coffee two-cup addict, it seemed the least he could do for her.

With breakfast eaten and the plates scraped, he decided it would be prudent for him to begin the rinsing of the dishes while Sophie went to clean her teeth. As he filled the sink up with fresh water and soap, he started washing the pans and crockery.

"You cook *and* clean?" Sophie exclaimed on returning back to the kitchen, raising one hand theatrically to her head, "be still my heart! You must be a gem among men!"

Artemais laughed.

"My brothers and I take turns, one cooks, another cleans, and we rotate through the days. I am a very house-trained male, never fear."

Sophie laughed, so Artemais decided now would be the best time to broach his question.

"Have you seen a doctor yet, Soph?"

He noticed her still, like a deer caught in headlights.

"I was going to yesterday, but between quitting and eating a mountain of ice cream I never made it. Why?"

Artemais stacked the last dish on the drying rack and wiped his hands on the tea towel. Gently clasping both her shoulders in his hands he looked down into her face.

"Just wondering, love. Nothing sinister. I am under the illusion that it is standard procedure to get a general checkup from the doctor once you realize you're pregnant, right?"

When she nodded, he smiled.

"Then let's make the appointment. I don't want anything bad to happen to my little man in there."

Sophie released her breath.

"I'm sorry, Artemais, I know you didn't mean it as a personal remark. I think I'm a tad grouchy first thing in the mornings."

He laughed and kissed the tip of her nose. He couldn't resist.

"You? Never! Come on—make the phone call and I'll come with you—I'd like to see my son."

Sophie rolled her eyes and bit down on her lip to keep herself from pointing out her child wasn't necessarily a boy. She knew he would listen politely and then continue to refer to their child as male anyway. She might as well pick her battles.

Dialing the phone, she rebooked her appointment for later that morning. Hanging up, she waved him into the bathroom.

"Go on. Get cleaned up and we can head on out. We can walk from here, the fresh air might do us both good."

Artemais quickly gave her a most chaste and fleeting kiss, then hurried into the sanctity of the bathroom before she could complain of his taking liberties. He liked this side of his mate, the grouchy, first-thing-in-the-morning rumpled look. He would never have guessed she had this side to her from what he had seen.

She was full of surprises and he couldn't wait to unearth more.

Chapter Nine

Sophie twisted her head and shoulders back once again to look at the large ultrasound monitor and equipment attached.

"Relax, love. I'm sure the nurse has done this a number of times before."

Sophie pouted.

"I don't care. I'm not certain I trust this. I mean, what if the machine fries itself and hurts the baby? What if the ultrasound waves hurt her? What if she's sensitive — or, oh my gosh! — what if she's allergic to something? What if it hurts her?"

"Shh… I'm not going to let anything hurt you, Soph. Trust me. We've already asked that poor Doctor a zillion and one questions. She assured us everything was above board and nothing would hurt the baby."

Sophie bit down on her lip. She knew she was being stupid, but she couldn't help but worry. She twisted back to look at the handle-like object connected to the monitor.

"I still don't like it. I'm not sure we should be doing this."

Before Artemais could start pulling at his hair, a nurse walked through the curtain, obviously overhearing her comment.

"Don't worry Mrs. Rutledge, I promise we do this every day. There aren't any adverse reactions or effects. It's all perfectly safe."

"I'm not—"

Artemais squeezed her hand, tightly, so she cut off her words.

The nurse smiled soothingly, obviously used to calming half-hysterical mothers-to-be every day. Sophie mumbled under her breath something to the effect of cursing all men and the problems they bear upon their women. Artemais ignored the implied thrust to his ego and manhood. He simply felt too excited to be catching the first glimpse of his son.

The nurse told Sophie to raise her shirt and pull her jeans below her hips, baring her abdomen, then smeared a healthy dollop of conductive gel onto the handle of the ultrasound.

Artemais held Sophie's hand as she squealed her protests of the chilly gel on her warm skin. It took all his control and effort not to laugh aloud at her girlish complaints.

Five minutes later the nurse turned the monitor so they could both easily see the screen.

"There's your baby. It's too early to determine it's gender, but in a couple of months time we should be able to get a decent look—if we're lucky and baby here cooperates by positioning itself correctly."

Artemais looked carefully and the black and white grainy images on the screen. He and Sophie studied the image intensely. The more he looked, the clearer the grainy image appeared. He could detect the head, and the blob of the rest of the body.

His son was so tiny!

Artemais felt tears gather in his eyes, and he blinked rapidly, trying to force them away. His mouth hung partially open, and he could no longer resist. He stepped forward, right up to the side of Sophie's bed and leaned over her, to touch the screen.

Delicately, as if the screen were made of a soap bubble and to hurt it would shatter his son, he oh-so-lightly ran his fingers up and down his son.

"My boy." He stated simply, completely overcome by the moment.

For once, Sophie did not retort her beliefs on the gender of their child.

Snapping back to reality, he realized that he could merely *see* his son on this screen, but all this was actually inside his Sophie. The instant the thought took hold he looked down at his woman, his mate. This woman bore his child.

He grinned, and looked down at her gel-smeared stomach. He swirled a few patterns in the jelly on her abdomen, reaching from just below her breasts to just above the line of her lower curls.

"Thank you, Sophie. Thank you for sharing this with me."

He noticed a suspicious wetness to Sophie's eyes also. As she was not mentioning the moisture in his, he refrained from teasing her. They simply stared at each other for a moment of simple understanding. They both cared for each other, and they both loved their child with all that was in them. They both wanted to protect it, cherish it and raise a happy, healthy baby. Nothing else seemed important when compared to that.

* * * * *

Sophie had forgotten how uncomfortable the hospital cot was, how the crick in her neck ached from staring back at the ultrasound monitor, even how annoyed and scared she felt with all this machinery and sick-people stuff surrounding her. Her fears this might adversely affect her little baby flitted on the edges of her mind, but she firmly squashed them.

All she could see was the touching love and devotion *radiating* from Artemais. If she had entertained even the *smallest* of doubts for his love and caring towards this baby, they were now set at rest. She knew with that natural instinct she came to listen to more and more, this man loved their baby, was *devoted* to the health and well-being of this baby. In this sense, she fully trusted him.

Unfortunately, this brought up a few tricky questions. If Artemais loved this baby, she had no right to deny him or the baby a happy, full relationship. Now she merely needed to know if Artemais could care for her apart from their child. Not an easy feat to work out. That would require trust, and probably much more time spent together.

Sophie looked deep into Artemais' eyes. He had taken the first steps. He had stuck by her, even when his brothers left them to head back to his precious home. That had been a step of faith and trust and commitment from him. Surely she could return the favor? Just because she would come to spend a week or two out in *his* natural environment didn't mean she was caving in, surely?

Sophie scrunched her face in thought. All relationships were two-way streets, and so far everything had gone her way. Artemais had found *her*—she hadn't gone looking for him. Artemais had stayed *with her*—she hadn't budged an inch for him. Artemais was here *with her*, holding her hand and soothing her fears about the evils of the ultrasound and promising to do battle with all sorts of nasty looking machinery to keep their baby safe.

What exactly had she done for him? Been stupid enough to miss a pill and fall pregnant? Have the well-meaning intention of looking him up in the near future to casually inform him he would be siring a baby?

Sophie berated herself. She was stronger than this! He had no right to insist she move house and cater to his whim—but so far he hadn't offered her anything permanent! He had merely asked her to come back to his place to make life simpler for him so they could get to know each other.

Sophie barely registered the nurse freezing the ultrasound screen and mumbling, "I'll leave you two to chat to your baby," and exited the small space.

Sophie took another look at her child, her daughter. She was such a tiny, itsy thing sleeping and growing inside her. Sophie figured that she deserved to get to know Artemais much better, not just for her own peace of mind, but also for their baby.

"If I don't like your place, do you swear to let me come back here? Come home?"

Artemais looked carefully at her, obviously weighing his words.

"I trust you to take some time, to let us get to know each other. I know we don't know each other very intimately," at her blush he hastily continued, "or at least know each other's personalities very intimately. I just want us to make the best go of this possible. I always assumed to have a family unit much like I had myself as a child, two parents, many children, lots of noise and fuss in the house. I'd like to think we're both mature enough and we care enough for each other to *try* and make this work."

Sophie nodded.

"Let's try. But we can drive up in my car, so I have a means of transportation. I've never stayed long in the country. It might drive me mad with boredom."

Artemais grinned a toothy, half-feral grin she knew she would soon adore and make her melt every time.

"I promise you, Soph. You won't be bored for long. Something is always happening around our place."

She nodded. Looking back to the monitor, she nearly spoke again when the nurse came in.

She smiled. "Seen enough?"

Sophie laughed. "Never. Can you print that out? So we can take it back with us and show my partner's brothers?"

The nurse looked at Artemais and nearly drooled.

"Of course."

Artemais looked at Sophie and winked.

"Baby's first photo. The boys will be totally stoked to see it. We might need to stop off at a copy shop before we drive back to make duplicates."

Sophie laughed, feeling lighthearted for the first time in a while. She and Artemais were going to try to make things work, she might even have another few chances to try for that incredible sex again and her tiny baby was happy, healthy and safe.

"Maybe we should make a number of photos. I might want a couple myself. One for my handbag, one for the mantelpiece, one for my bedroom…"

Laughing at Artemais' wry expression she tried to choke her giggles down. Taking his hand, she let him help her off the hospital cot.

"One thing at a time sweetheart, hmm?"

Chapter Ten

Sophie tried hard not to doze in the car on the way to Artemais' house. It was late afternoon and she felt physically and emotionally wrung out. After making six copies of the grainy ultrasound photo and tucking away the original in her little keepsakes box on her desk, she and Artemais had ordered in pizza and New York style cheesecake to celebrate.

They dined heartily, laughing and swapping stories, guzzling milk and exchanging more and more outrageous first-date stories. They were having a blast, one-upping each other until a particularly unpleasant story of Artemais' — explaining why he could never look at green silk dresses in the same manner again — "*Can you imagine how well it covers vomit when your date drinks too much and then tries dancing in stilettos to the band's music?*" This particularly unpleasant story had her clutching her stomach to stop her laughter, tears streaming down her cheeks.

When Sophie felt her stomach roll uncomfortably she tried to work out if she had merely laughed too hard, or swallowed her latest piece of double salami-double olive-extra cheese pizza incorrectly. When her stomach roiled again, she nearly choked on her sip of milk, desperate to settle her stomach.

Artemais, noting her distress had abruptly halted his story.

"Soph? You okay?"

She nodded, gasping for breath.

"I think I laughed too hard while swallowing the milk, or maybe the pizza."

She closed her eyes, desperate to stop the world spinning and her stomach gurgling.

In that instant, she knew she was going to be sick. Again.

Afternoon sickness! Her brain finally began working again.

"Oh shit."

Jumping up, her woolen sock-clad feet slipping slightly on her floorboards, she raced towards the bathroom.

Flinging the door open, she barely made it to the toilet in time. Retching helplessly, she emptied her stomach.

She could feel Artemais behind her, hear him wringing out another washcloth, much like he had yesterday. Without even being told she held out her hand to accept it. Wiping her face, she sat down on the tiles.

"You really shouldn't be here, watching this. It is *so* humiliating."

"Hey, I helped get you here, the least I can do is suffer with you. Anyway, surely I deserve some punishment for taking all the pleasure and none of the pain?"

Sophie opened one eye a crack.

"Damn straight," she instantly agreed, "You can cop one for mankind. But for now, I think I'm going to be sick again."

Sophie turned back to hug the porcelain, feeling wretched as her stomach tried vainly to wring out whatever was offending it so.

Minutes later, she sat back, shivering. She hated throwing up. Artemais gently released his hold on her, wiped her face and started the shower running.

"No more pizza for lunch, my sweet. I think soup and toast, maybe some noodles or something will be the order of the day until your sickness has passed. We can pig out during our dinners. I don't like seeing you hurt like this. Okay?"

Too wrung out to argue for the moment, Sophie nodded and let Artemais strip her down. She was grateful he didn't caress her, or act the seductive lover in any manner. She felt like shit and felt certain she looked worse. As if she were a child, he helped her into the shower, then called out his intentions of getting her a change of clothes.

Sounded just fine to her.

After a long, hot, steamy shower, she felt refreshed, but exhausted. She was grateful when Artemais helped her pack a rucksack full of clothes, adding in a number of her pregnancy books from her satchel. She thought wistfully of doing a search online for a book titled *101 Ways to Avoid Morning Sickness* and chuckled when the only helpful advice she could think of revolved around "Rule #1: DON'T GET PREGNANT".

Less than an hour later they were packed into her little Suzuki and on their way.

Chapter Eleven

Artemais could barely breathe. He had been driving for nearly an hour with Sophie lying sleepily next to him, both of them crammed into her small Suzuki. Her scent and the nearness of her soft body gave him a massive hard-on that nothing seemed to be relieving.

The mental picture of their tiny baby seemed etched into his memory, lay over his heart. But superimposed over all this were the many facets of Sophie. Sophie laughing at his horror stories, Sophie guzzling milk, Sophie looking worried, maybe even scared, at all the instruments near the ultrasound. She had so many different sides, so many different faces that she wore, he found the more he uncovered the more he wanted to see of her, learn of her.

He had been entertaining thoughts of seducing her after lunch, had been directing the conversation gently towards their chemistry, the intensity of their reaction to each other when she had become sick. He felt awful about his selfish, horny thoughts, yet he just couldn't help himself.

Her scent—that light, flowery, mossy scent that reminded him of freedom and the outdoors—it was slowly driving him mad.

He had been wearing his hard-on for at least an hour and a half, since leaving the doctor's, after seeing his son's picture. He cringed when he thought of how long previous to that he had been aroused for. And if he counted the previous six weeks where he had been slowly driving himself mental over his erotic dream-sharing with her...if he didn't get to release himself inside her soon he was a doomed man.

To make him feel worse, it seemed obvious to him his mate needed a nap, a decent sleep, and here he was, lewdly thinking of all the ways and positions he wanted to take her, both inside the small car, outside leaning up against the trunk or door, or even outside on the lush forest floor. Guilt made him feel a thousand times worse than his aching cock ever could.

He had fallen silent some time ago, as Sophie's eyes struggled to remain open. Gently, he had told her it would be a decent drive and she should try to get some rest. Mumbling incoherently she had resisted until the lulling of the car had let her fall into a light sleep.

Leaving Artemais with his lusty thoughts and super-hardened cock.

Left to his own thoughts and musings, each and every thought had come back to this woman next to him, about how much he desired her, how desperately he wished to plunge himself deep into her soft body. And more. He wanted to talk to her forever, share his amusing stories and hear about her life, hear her thoughts and opinions on a million small matters.

He wanted to spend his life with her, both physically and mentally.

As they wound their way up the dirt track that eventually led to his driveway, Sophie's eyes fluttered.

He could see her trying to focus on the passing greenery, the leafy, heavy foliage of the forest. Even through the car he could smell the scent of the wildness outside, surrounding them. A totally different wildness to the one building inside him.

"Good afternoon, Sunshine. Feeling better?"

Artemais tried his best not to chuckle at the way she blearily rubbed her eyes, like an infant waking from a nap.

"Are we there yet?"

Artemais could no longer hold his chuckle inside.

"Fifteen, twenty minutes tops. I haven't been driving overly fast as I didn't want to wake you up. I figured pregnant women needed all the sleep they could manage. I must have read that somewhere."

"Why are you laughing?"

"Sorry, love. You just made me think of a little kid, waking after its nap. It was an amusing thought."

Artemais laughed even harder when she stuck her tongue out at him and looked out the window. Before he could tease her further, she changed the topic.

"Where exactly are we?"

Artemais swallowed his laughter, enjoying their play.

"Currently we're running along the outside edge of Glacier National Park. Our house is on the other side, backing in to it. As you can see, it's a truly beautiful, densely populated Park. There's a small village a couple of miles down the other side, away from the Parkland. That's where we do most of our grocery shopping. It's a small village, maybe fifty or so residents. Everyone knows everyone, so it's nice and safe."

Artemais described many of the residents, all of whom had a hand somehow raising him and his brothers. A few new men and women had come and gone over the years, but he told her of their antics as youths to make her chuckle.

For the most part, he had little idea of what he said. Sophie's sparkling gray eyes rested on him, drinking him in. Her soft curls fluffed around her features in a just-got-out-of-bed manner that drove him wild. With the weak sun shining down through the windshield, he felt his temperature rise until he feared he would explode. He wanted Sophie and he wanted her now.

From the small smile her face cocked into, and the wicked glint reflected in her eyes, he *knew* she knew what he thought about, what he desperately craved. She winked cheekily at him as he explained how one of the residents had chased Dominic from a window with a broom for trying to "seduce" his pretty twenty-year-old cousin on leave from college. He stumbled to a halt, completely enchanted. Sophie giggled at him.

"Sounds to me like everyone knows what deliciously horny young men you all are."

He raised an eyebrow to that comment, daring her to elaborate on the sparks they both knew were flying.

"Well, seriously! What women can resist such beefcake spread before her? Even cut short, your hair is soft and a divine color, your eyes fairly scream sex and soft pillow talk, and secrets shared. Your body…"

Artemais grinned as she trailed off, flushing slightly.

"Well, suffice to say I understand why women the world over would find it hard to resist any one of you."

"Any one of us?" he pressed.

Sophie merely glared at him, and he chuckled.

"I refuse to feed your ego even more."

"Sophie, love, it's not my ego I want you to feed."

He laughed harder when Sophie looked down to the huge tent his jeans were straining to become. Wearing a hard-on in jeans was the most uncomfortable thing he had ever experienced.

"Well, true enough. But I don't relish the thought of bedroom gymnastics in this little car. One of us would end up in hospital. I suppose you're going to have to be a little patient, aren't you?"

Artemais took his eyes from the road and stared at her. The sensual promise in her eyes, the wicked, *knowing* glint rocked him to his very core. She knew how desperately he craved her, and she simply smiled over it, accepting of it.

Artemais pressed his foot on the accelerator, feeling pleasure as the little Suzuki responded and lurched forward faster, no doubt about it—the small car had guts and determination. He ignored Sophie's tinkling laugh, as the scent of her, that delicious scent emanating from her core, surrounded him and drove his lust higher.

The quicker he got Sophie home, the quicker he could kiss her. And the quicker he could kiss her, the quicker he could drag her into his part of the house, lock the door and…cursing his heating blood and hugely straining cock, he took the turns in the road faster than he should have. Finally he saw the dirt entrance to his driveway.

With dirt spewing from under the tires of the small car, he made the last turn into their driveway.

It would be five minutes, ten tops, 'til he could drag her out of the car and into his house. As long as his brothers didn't get in the way, he was finally home.

Chapter Twelve

Artemais pulled the handbrake on the little Suzuki, relieved to finally be home with his woman, but frustrated beyond belief that she could so easily destroy his control. Even as she sat next to him in the passenger seat, half turned towards him, he could see the laughter lighting her beautiful gray eyes.

"In a rush? Are we being chased by demons from hell? Or maybe vampires?"

Artemais growled, a low rumble through his chest. Sophie might be laughing at him, and deep inside he also laughed at himself, but at this moment, he felt very harshly done by. It was taking every iota of his legendary control to not pull her on top of him, tear her jeans away from her body and release himself, plunging his huge rock-hard cock into her wetness.

Sophie must have seen some indication of his level of lust in his eyes, or maybe his growl of need reached her at some level. She removed her seat belt and laid a cool hand on his arm.

"Hey, don't worry. Your presence has been driving me nuts too. This…thing we have between us — it's strange isn't it?"

"Not that strange. Not to my people. We need to talk Sophie; I need to tell you some stuff. But first, we have to go inside and I have to be with you or I think I'll lose my mind."

"I thought it was the woman who struck fear into the man's heart by saying those words, 'We have to talk'. They really do sound ominous. Do you mind very much if we have mind-blowing sex first, and talk seriously afterwards, when we both might be able to concentrate for any length of time? I'm sure it'll be much easier for us both that way."

Artemais nodded and opened the car door, coming around the other side for Sophie.

He took her hand and started purposefully towards the front door of the house — the closest entrance to his part of the large house. Sophie was staring at his house, but he briefly apologized and pulled her up to the porch, too eager to get her inside to show his pride for his ancestral home.

Just as he was about to climb onto the large front porch, his eyes fell onto the front windows of his office. A large, sunny room, his office always stood open to all of his siblings, any time they required to use the space. All his laptops, surveillance prototypes and other bits and pieces from work were kept in the large room. He used it as his headquarters when he was home. The company offices themselves were back in the main city.

This afternoon, all three of his brothers appeared to be having a powwow, and all three were now pressed up against the window, looking at him and Sophie like kids at a candy store.

The knowledge that his brothers would jump on them the instant they entered the house, commandeer Sophie to chat and charm her, washed over him. His fantasies of having a few quiet hours with her, relearning her body, her scent, wallowing in their mutual explorations flew away in a puff of smoke.

He felt like howling his dismay. His brothers meant well, but privacy was not a strong commodity around here. Flings, casual affairs, those had privacy. A mate, particularly his mate, the first woman to join their family since their mother died, would in itself negate any privacy he had hoped for.

Making his mind up in an instant, he stopped where he was. Sophie paused beside him, not having noticed his brothers. She was eagerly looking around the large house and gardens.

Artemais smote his brothers with a glare. As the eldest, he had felt responsible for his brothers until they all reached adulthood. The glare he gave them was not a new one for them. It reminded them *he* was the eldest and *he* was in charge.

The three brotherly grins that came from that glare were taunting and feral. A clear challenge. Artemais frowned again, growling low in his throat. William, the first to truly understand, touched the shoulders of Samuel and Dominic, saying something to them. Both brothers turned back to look at him again. They both nodded, then smiled brilliantly.

"Later," he saw them mouth through the glass. He nodded, realizing he could only gain a semblance of privacy for himself and Sophie. The rest he would deal with later.

His brothers taken care of, and knowing they would never dare to follow him out into the woods, Artemais turned abruptly.

"Change of plans," he curtly told Sophie.

Keeping his pace at a stride Sophie could keep up with, Artemais headed towards the huge forest surrounding the house. He knew once his brothers had finished inundating Sophie with questions they would slip back into the background, allowing them some measure of privacy. But as hot and horny as he felt, he couldn't trust himself to wait that long.

He needed his mate now.

Chapter Thirteen

Sophie stared at the truly enormous house that would undoubtedly be one of her baby's homes. Still undecided about whether she could live with Artemais, or whether she should hold out and try to convince him to live in the city with her, she pushed the thought back in into the dark depths of her mind.

Instead, she concentrated on the truly beautiful house in front of her. Made of brick and wood, it had a comfy, homey look to it, even though it stood three stories tall and could compete with some mansions she knew.

There was obviously more than enough room to raise a passel full of children, her mind hinted strongly. Pushing aside that wistful thought, she let her eyes soak up the huge old house.

She could only partially see all the space around the back of the house. The front garden was fairly barren, but huge. Around the edges was heaps of room to plant a vegetable garden, or maybe some flowers. The grass overflowed everywhere, soft and safe for babies to learn to walk, run and play everywhere.

She barely noticed when Artemais stopped just shy of climbing the stairs up onto the porch. The house seemed perfectly maintained; evidently the boys had taken their family home seriously. Only the gardens looked neglected, and even then, the ground was safe, the grass fairly well cut. It appeared more neglected from her woman's perspective—with no flowers, no vegetables, nothing decorative except the healthy green of the grass.

The lawn was neatly trimmed, the weeds were only straggling around the edges, not completely overrunning the garden. It was the bareness that offended her feminine pride, in her mind's eye she knew how magnificent this garden *could* look, and so its bareness became an eyesore to her, personally.

Before she could question Artemais on why no one had given time or love to the garden, he began pulling her in another direction, around the back of the house.

Laughing, she followed where he led.

"What is this? I thought you were all hot and ready to jump my bones? Did you forget something important you needed to show me?"

Artemais grunted.

"No. My brothers were waiting to ambush us. It would have been hours before I could drag you away. But I'm adaptable, I just decided on a small change in the plans."

Sophie shook her head and chuckled at him.

Five minutes later, Artemais led her into a small clearing, the beauty of which stole her breath away.

A thin brook trickled by the side of the clearing. The grass was so lush and green it looked as soft and comfortable as moss. With huge old trees towering over them, Sophie could well imagine this clearing looking the same down through the past thousand years. Purple and blue wildflowers grew beside the stream, and Sophie could tell simply by the way Artemais' shoulders had relaxed, and his breathing had softened that this was a special, private place for him to relax and think.

She wasn't surprised at all when he dragged her into

his arms and kissed her fiercely. She had dreamed of this man for weeks, remembered every heated caress, every deep, drugging kiss. She had fantasized about him every single night. Closing her eyes, she leaned into his heat and let herself get lost in his mouth.

After a moment of blissful passion, he pulled back slightly, breathing heavily. Still dazed, she could only listen to his words.

"Do you have any idea how often I dreamt of this these last few weeks? How every night I would taste you again? Feel you again? Be driven insane by your caress? Only to wake up cold and alone?" His words came from deep in his soul.

Sophie shuddered, tempted beyond belief by the seductive quality of his voice. She knew what he felt, could feel the truth in his words and conviction in his heart. He wanted her and if the seductive tone of his voice and heat in his words were any indication he would be a formidable opponent.

While she might convince herself she could hold him at bay for a time while she learned more about him and their situation, she was not a fool, and knew that her body would not be able to resist his seduction for long.

Sophie groaned, feeling herself grow damp at the heat and desperation his words and her thoughts brought. Giving in to her body's desperate desire, she gave herself fully into their kiss. In that moment, nothing else mattered except his mouth, his tongue thrusting in and out of her, teasing her, beckoning her, tempting her.

Arching herself up into Artemais' heat, she felt his hugely erect cock, and rubbed herself against it.

They both groaned.

Without letting her mouth go, Artemais guided her down onto the soft mossy ground, and lifted her shirt. Palming her nipple through her lacy bra, he groaned as it instantly became erect.

"Oh my," she gasped, trying to keep a hold of her thoughts, trying to make sense of her instant, hot reaction. The memories of her erotic dreams superimposed themselves over her memories of that one night. Her brain brought forth a million erotic ideas of what she could do, what Artemais could do to her to drive her wild.

Determined to simply not follow his lead, Sophie decided to up the stakes a little. If Artemais could palm her nipples, she too could explore his stunning body.

Lowering her hands, she swiftly unbuckled his belt and opened his fly. She dipped her hand into his briefs, and gently, but firmly clasped his massively hard cock in her hand.

Sophie barely registered that Artemais had stopped his playing, so focused had she been on the warmth and strength of his cock. She could circle his width in her hand, but only just. He was long, and purely, beautifully masculine. While she was no blushing virgin, Sophie felt awed by Artemais' length. They had been so caught up in the moment that night, so desperate to wildly fuck each other they had never taken to time to get to know each other softly.

In that moment, Sophie swore to herself that very, very soon she would take some time to learn Artemais in a softer, more intimate manner.

For now, however, merely touching him drove up her lust, making her wish for nothing else but for him to plunge himself inside her, taking her over and over again.

Knowing that she was a few well-placed strokes away from coming, having undergone a six-week personal foreplay session each night, Sophie figured it well past time to get the ball rolling with Artemais, as he merely stared down at her, mouth agape at the liberties she was taking.

Stroking his hot length, up and down a few times, she scooted down his body so her mouth rested near his cock.

Breathing softly over him, letting the heat of her mouth rest just a small thrust away, Sophie smiled and looked up the length of Artemais' body to catch his eye.

The blue of his eyes had darkened, so instead of being the rich, clear blue of a summer sky, they now were the deep, royal blue of twilight, just before darkness overtook the earth.

Sophie grinned at the strange way her mind worked. If her analogy were true, then *she* was the darkness about to take over her lover.

As her mouth enclosed the head of his cock, Artemais growled his approval low in his throat. Sophie palmed his soft balls, wishing she had the patience to truly take her time here. But her intentions were to drive Artemais to the brink and let them both take their pleasure now.

She left his balls to cup her hands around his cock. Sucking fiercely, she began to pump his length.

Before she could even set up a rhythm, Artemais had grabbed her shoulders and pulled her back up. Briefly worrying about grass stains, Sophie grinned cockily as he held her in place by lowering himself to trap her from the waist down.

"What's wrong? Didn't you like my ministrations?"

"Honey, after six weeks of erotic dreams that have

been driving me nuts, no way am I letting you suck me off first time around. What say we save that for the third or fourth go about? Hmm?"

Effectively silenced at the thought of having three or four orgasms this afternoon, Sophie simply stared up at this man. She would have questioned his inflated ego, if she didn't know he had so much stamina. So that night hadn't been some fluke or release of a long celibacy? Then how could he get erect so fast?

Artemais kissed her with a fierce, pent-up passion, effectively halting her thoughts. Arching up into him, Sophie fumbled, trying to grasp him once more.

"No Soph, don't. If you do, this won't last more than a second."

"I want you right now, Artemais. I don't want the pretty words or the sentiment. I've been dreaming of you every night. Six weeks of foreplay is enough, don't you think? I won't break, just do it now."

Artemais growled his approval and ripped her shirt up over her head. The sunshine speckling through the trees helped lend some heat against the chilly breeze that had her nipples peaking again. When Artemais' mouth closed over one of her nipples, Sophie suddenly felt too warm, too hot.

"Artemais," she cried out, arching into him, desperately seeking some relief.

"Did you think of this?" he growled out, hungry for more of her reactions, "Did you think of me taking this nipple? Suckling it? Taking your clit? While I was looking for you? Waiting for you?"

Not even waiting for her answer, he pushed his jeans off his legs and left them on the moss. Not missing a beat, he thrust his hand down her silky panties to lightly flick her engorged clit. Crying out, she arched up into his hand, his mouth, the heat of his possession.

Stroking her, crooning to her, Artemais drove her up to her peak, then bent his head, sucking her clit into his mouth. Gently, but firmly, he bit down onto it, forcing her over her climax. Crying out her pleasure, writhing in the grass, Sophie was incoherent in her passion.

Catching her breath, she started unbuttoning Artemais' shirt. Fumbling, she tore a few buttons, scattering them on the ground. As he lifted his head, she caught his gaze with her own flushed face.

"I need you now," she choked out, "hot, hard, inside me now."

Instantly, his lazy gaze turned sharp and hot. He shoved her jeans down, fully off her legs, taking her panties with them. As Sophie finally got his shirt free, Artemais had discarded his briefs. They both stared at each other for a second. Each soaked up the beauty of the other, thanking God for the perfection of their lover.

Spreading her legs wide, Artemais fondled Sophie's damp slit, checking one last time she truly was ready for him and enjoyed the way she cried out, arched into his hand. When she grabbed his arm, pulling him down on top of her, he knew she felt too impatient to need any more foreplay.

"Now," she murmured, demandingly, confirming his suspicion.

Eager as she, he held himself still for half a moment, enjoying the tense excitement of this moment; then he thrust directly into her in one long, fierce, claiming lunge.

She was tight.

She was hot.

And she was so wet he nearly came there and then.

Kissing her fiercely, he palmed her nipple, tweaking it and enjoying the cries of delight she made. Thrusting into her, slowly and steadily, he breathed deeply, willing himself to last.

"Now," she cried, writhing. "I don't need you to be gentle Artemais. I need you *now!*" she demanded, scratching his back.

The slight pain made him lose any semblance of control he had retained, and he thrust harder, deeper, on the verge of climaxing. His loss of control seemed to spur her on, making her climax once more. He roared his release, throwing himself after her.

Spending himself inside her, feeling his seed shoot deeply into her, reminded him that Sophie was bearing his child, his son. Sophie was his true mate in all ways. Lying down on top of her while he caught his breath, he enjoyed this rare moment of total peace, here in his favorite spot in the woods, with his woman.

Snuggling down next to her, the soft moss acting as a thin blanket against the hard dirt beneath them, Artemais cupped Sophie to him. Inhaling her scent, he felt himself stir once more.

Gently pulling himself out from her, he rested his head down in her soft, blonde curls. Mixed with the myriad scents in the wild woods out here, Sophie's scent blended in perfectly with the scents of the wild.

She belongs here, he thought, *she fits here perfectly, just as I do, just as my brothers do, just as the Pack does.*

Hugging her tightly to him, cradling her to him, he stopped that dangerous train of thought before he went too far. It would be Sophie's choice. He would use everything he could to keep her here with him, but ultimately it needed to be her choice to stay here with him, to become his family.

You can't hold something that refused to be kept, he knew. He needed to convince Sophie that she *wanted* to be here, to be kept by him.

When Sophie unexpectedly snuggled deeper into his embrace, nuzzling his chest and shoulder, he felt his cock harden immediately. He had always been a randy man, but something about Sophie made him worse than ever. Insatiable was not a boast.

As Sophie nuzzled him, her scent covered him, seemed to seep into his very pores and settle there for good. Slowly, Artemais started stroking her once more, with no intention but to soothe her. Gently he kneaded her arms, her back, relaxing her muscles and simply enjoying his touch upon her skin. She shivered and stretched up to kiss him.

Slowly exploring her mouth, in no hurry, he felt a little surprised when she slid her tongue into his mouth, to tease and caress his tongue.

She had never taken the initiative with him, and her small gesture had him instantly hard all over again. Artemais fought to restrain his wild urges. If his Sophie wanted to seduce him, he sure as hell wouldn't ruin it for her — no matter how hot and wild it drove him.

Gently at first, and then with growing urgency, he tangled his tongue with hers. *Maybe just a slight push*, he thought, *just to let her know how much I want her*. When Sophie rolled him over onto his back and straddled his waist he bit back a moan, knowing she wanted to seduce him and lead the pace this time around. He hoped it wouldn't kill him.

Sophie pulled her mouth away from his, and he looked up at her. The late afternoon sunshine speckled through the trees, casting shadows and forming a golden halo around her curls. Firming his decision to let her set the pace, Artemais clenched his fists down by his side and breathed deeply. Catching her eye, he raised an eyebrow mockingly.

"You set the pace this time love, I indulged myself last time."

* * * * *

Sophie grinned. He'd *indulged* himself with her, had he? Well, he might make her shiver and melt with that wicked tongue of his, he might make her want to moan and writhe with his touch, but she felt confidant she could still hold her own against him.

His tenderness and obvious care for her made her feel invincible. She could leap tall buildings, dodge bullets — she felt certain she could seduce this man and make him insensate with lust and longing. Plus it would be incredible fun to do.

Grinning to herself at her wickedly wanton thoughts, she wriggled, positioned herself so her mound rested just below his balls. It was the perfect position for her to lean over him, cover the length of his torso with her own body and nibble at his nipples.

Slowly, taking her own sweet time, she wetly kissed the erect little nubs and ran her fingers through the light, springy hair that covered his chest. Whisper-soft, she raked her nails through the hair, enough to cause a sensation, but not enough to mark his skin or hurt.

Swirling her fingers, creating patterns at random, she enticed him, teased him while giving him some pleasure, just knowing it was not nearly enough. Slowly at first, and then more and more rapidly as she nibbled and teased his nipples, she listened as Artemais' breathing began to come in pants. She wiggled her bottom slightly, pretending to get a better position, and enjoyed feeling the rock hardness of him. His cock strained, his balls were raised and heavy — just how she liked her man.

Gently meandering, she let her hands circle lower and lower. Teasingly, she skimmed his hipbone, only to rise back to his abs. When both her hands ran over his lower belly, giving only the merest caress to the head of his cock as they passed over its tip, she finally elicited the groan she sought from Artemais.

"Something wrong, Artemais?"

Not even expecting him to answer, Sophie smiled at the stoic expression on his face. When faced with such manly stubbornness, what else was a girl to do but try to wring the biggest response possible from her adorable lover?

Pulling out the big guns, Sophie slid down his body a few more inches. Wetly, she kissed down the centerline of his chest. Slowly, with nibbles here and there, still caressing and lightly scoring his chest, Sophie meandered her way down his chest, heading towards the hugely straining cock.

As she halted, the base of her chin just a hairbreadth away from the tip of his cock, Sophie felt a thrill of success as Artemais canted his hips unconsciously, begging silently for her to take him.

Cupping his balls, Sophie looked up the length of his body. Face flushed, eyes wild, Artemais watched her, fists clenched at his side. He was biting his lip, holding himself back in every way, waiting for her pleasure. Something about having this strong, large man at her mercy made her smile hugely, eyes brightening with joy.

"Sophie," he growled, part plea, part warning.

She tried to place an innocent expression on her face, but she suspected the large grin threatening to split her mouth ruined the effect.

She turned her head back and took him into her mouth, as deeply as she could comfortably go without choking. They both groaned—at the pleasure, at the heat. Sophie sucked him deep into her mouth, swiping her tongue over his head and swallowing the tiny pearls of pre-cum.

Wrapping the rest of his length firmly within her grasp, she slowly, gently, started caressing him, pumping him. She worked as slowly as she dared. She didn't want his ardor to cool, but she did want to drag these moments out as long as possible.

Teasing him, she laved his head, pumped his cock, then looked up to his face. Artemais' eyes were now squeezed tightly shut, his head thrown back in pleasure. His nails dug into his palms, clenched at his side.

Sophie started playing gently with his balls, rolling the sac in her hands, lightly flicking her nail along the soft under-skin.

In a rush, Artemais reached for her and drew her head down onto his cock more deeply. "Please, Soph. Finish me."

Sophie grinned around his cock. Their silent game of chicken had paid off. Artemais looked half-wild with his lust. His eyes burned with lust and desire, his hips thrust his cock into her mouth. Feeling an answering dampness inside her, Sophie realized that by taking control of their lovemaking, she took control of herself in their relationship.

Releasing her mouth from his cock, she tried not to giggle at the moan of disappointment that came from Artemais.

"How do you taste on me?" she whispered.

Leaning forwards to kiss him fully, Sophie positioned herself above Artemais' straining cock. As she thrust her tongue into his mouth, sharing their combined flavor, she simultaneously thrust down onto his cock, impaling herself.

They both groaned in unison at their joining. Once again, Sophie led the pace, but this time there was no casual, teasing quality to it. She rode him hard, pushed both of them faster and faster as their breaths mingled and they gasped. As she clenched her inner muscles to grasp his cock even tighter, she felt the now-familiar tremble begin deep inside her womb.

Gasping, she felt lightheaded, heard the roaring in her ears. Meeting Artemais' deep, penetrating strokes, she rode through the crashing waves of their pleasure, and screamed. Vaguely, she felt his hands grasping her hips, pulling her down even harder onto his cock. She felt him erupt inside her, shooting jet after jet of his hot cum deep inside her. When the internal tremors subsided, she collapsed on Artemais' chest. She was sweating and still panting slightly as she caught her breath. Sophie felt much better with her cheek lying over Artemais' heartbeat, hearing it pumping furiously. She felt his warm arms circle around her and bring her close, holding her protectively in the curve of his body.

Sophie closed her eyes. She was safe and well here. Physical exhaustion washed through her and she let the safe darkness of sleep take over.

Chapter Fourteen

When Sophie stirred, Artemais shifted slightly. She wasn't heavy, but while she napped he had been deep in thought and now some of his rapidly cooling muscles complained.

He couldn't deny the huge feeling of possession welling inside him. He felt ecstatic that she trusted him enough to fall asleep on him, and he knew he could build slowly and carefully on this trust. After all, he had five or six months for them to get to know each other, to learn about each other. They were certainly in no rush right now.

Artemais felt a tug on his heart when Sophie sleepily raised her head and smiled down at him. Moving her hand to push her sleep-tousled curls from her eyes, he felt his heart beat faster. She looked adorable. When she laughed aloud and commented, "Don't you ever carry condoms?" he felt a slight shiver of warning.

He and his brothers had never been sick, never had any sort of human illness. Years ago his grandfather had explained that no werewolf in their pack for as far back as he could recall had ever carried a human disease. Most of the time, their immune systems were compatible with a human's.

While they didn't donate blood for fear of something being found in it upon close examination, ordinary pharmaceuticals such as painkillers seemed to work for a short time, their body simply burnt through the drugs much faster than a normal human.

Neither had a pack member ever caught an STD to their knowledge, and as only a true mate could be impregnated by an Alpha male, the need for condoms was only a smokescreen to not scare away the human women.

The first few times he had been with Sophie, Artemais had followed convention and worn the rubber. Yet as his certainty of Sophie being the one grew stronger, his desire to see her rounded with his child also grew, until finally he convinced himself to dispense with the condom.

Lucky for him.

Artemais felt weighted by his secrets from her. If he expected her to trust him and be honest with him, he needed to return the favor. He needed to tell her about himself and his Pack.

"Uh, there's a few things I need to tell you," he started, uncertain. Sophie didn't help matters. She simply watched him, waiting and expectant. She still had that glow about her; that just-been-satisfied look, and he really didn't want to ruin it.

"Well, now is probably a good time to start," she prodded.

Wondering if he should have read an etiquette book, to see if there were rules on how to tell a woman one was a werewolf, he faltered a minute. When doubt and concern started appearing in Sophie's eyes, he cursed himself.

Who needs tact? he decided.

"I'm a werewolf," he stated. "My brothers and I are the only remaining offspring of the Alpha male and female of the local pack. You're carrying my baby, who will inherit the title and someday rule the pack. You're my mate and the only woman who could possibly be mine in every way."

Artemais stopped as Sophie howled in laughter. The vibrations of her laughter echoed through him, and he wondered briefly if he should feel offended.

As Sophie continued laughing at him, starting up again each time she caught her breath and looked at him, Artemais sighed.

Finally, Sophie rolled off his chest to sit primly on the mossy bank. Her laughter had almost subsided; she now only hiccupped and giggled when she looked at his serious face.

He waited while she wiped the tears that streamed down her face. While a part of him felt quite offended at her laughter, the rational part of his brain couldn't really conjure up any anger.

He didn't have many close friends, other than his brothers, and so between them and the other few pack members, he had never needed to tell anyone about his moonlit romps and monthly changings.

In the back of his mind he had expected anger, disgust, many reactions, but laughter?

After a few more minutes, Sophie caught her breath, to see his slightly grumpy, slightly bewildered look. She finally shook herself slightly and flicked her curls from her eyes, completely unaware of the gloriously naked picture she made.

"You think you're serious, don't you? I must admit, I thought I'd heard every male excuse for not bringing condoms, but yours certainly is the most original I've heard."

From the choking noises coming from the back of her throat, Artemais would bet money she was trying hard not to dissolve into another fit of giggles. He sighed.

"I *am* serious. Do you really think I'd make something like this up, Sophie?"

Her brows crinkled in thought. "Well, it is kind of dumb. I mean, if there *really* were werewolves running around, surely we'd know?"

He sat up and leaned back.

"How?" he challenged her.

"Well," she thought a moment, "it's not like wolves are hugely populating the area. And if a stack of men really were changing into furry wolves on the night of the full moon," she choked down more laughter, desperately trying to be serious, "wouldn't we poor humans notice the great influx of wolves?"

Artemais shook his head.

"It's not like there's hundreds of us. Twenty-five years ago, my pack suffered a huge culling, killing more than half of us. There's only a dozen or so of us left, most of them elderly Beta men and women."

Instantly, he saw the concern and sorrow in her eyes.

"You were culled?"

"My parents, and grandmother were among them. Many old friends died too."

"Oh Artemais, I'm sorry." Sophie blinked when she realized what her words meant. Doubt and worry clouded her gaze.

"When is the next full moon?" she queried.

"Friday."

Sophie searched his face. He could tell she didn't know what to believe. Evidently she thought *he* believed what he said, but she wasn't convinced. Not that he could blame her.

"Is it…? Are you…? I mean…"

"I'd never be a danger to you, love. Surely you know that? You're my mate and I would protect you with my life." Dragging her close, he hugged her tight. He needed her to believe that much at least. When she sighed and snuggled trustingly into his chest, he hoped half the fight of her belief in him was won.

If he had really wanted to, he could have changed into a wolf there and then for her, but he thought he had pressed his luck as much as he could today. He knew the conversation held a lot for her to take in, and even though she only half believed him, the worst parts for him were over. He and his brothers could charm her into staying, and when she saw them on the full moon…well, hopefully she trusted him to keep her safe.

It was better than her screaming and running away in a panic. His Sophie certainly proved without a doubt her core held made of sterner stuff, he thought, filled with pride at the knowledge.

Chapter Fifteen

As Sophie drew her clothes back on, her mind whirled with stray thoughts. She had never made love in a public place before, and while this deserted, gorgeous woodlands area wasn't exactly public, and it certainly wasn't in a closed bedroom.

Anyone could have come across them, yet she had been far too engrossed, far too focused on Artemais and the exciting feelings he brought up in her to think about petty things like being caught like a couple of teenagers necking in a car.

What worried her more, though, was the niggling worry that she didn't know if she believed what Artemais was telling her or not. He looked so serious, so *very* serious that she knew *he* believed he was a werewolf. And this wasn't really something one could be mistaken in surely? It's not like one could turn into a wolf and *not* realize it?

Sophie shook her head, confused. When Artemais had been talking to her about being a werewolf, she recalled herself as a young child.

She had always been one of those children, down at the bottom of gardens and checking under mushrooms in parks, looking for fairies and goblins. Imagining she was a Queen in exile. She had never been girly enough to want to be a fairy princess, but she had dreamt that she came from another country, another world. She had always owned an amazing imagination, reading Enid Blyton and utterly charmed with the idea of being a changeling.

Her grandmother had caught her one afternoon, stomping her foot in exasperation, *demanding* the fairies come out and play. As her parents had died when she had been young, her beloved grandmother had raised her as best she could. She had been sat down on Grandmother's lap, and explained that while magic did exist, things like fairies and vampires, werewolves and goblins were never quite as the myths and tales told them.

Grandmother had never told her these things didn't exist, but she had pointed out that, just like in Chinese Whispers, a tale told more than once to different people changed, so did legends over time.

"For every Legend that persists, an element of truth is present," had been a saying that her grandmother had repeated often during those years. Sophie had clung to those words as a child. She had never really stopped believing that magic and fairies existed, but she had been skeptical on how vampires and werewolves could exist without general knowledge.

To her dismay, Sophie realized instead of running away, climbing back into her car and driving as far away as humanly possible, she instead wanted to ask Artemais a million questions. Her childlike curiosity had never really waned. Instead, it had lain dormant as she grew into adulthood.

Sophie blushed as Artemais winked at her. He, too, silently pulled his clothes back on. The rogue thought that such a gorgeous man shouldn't need to clothe himself swiftly followed with the desire to rip said clothes from him again and screw his brains out, right there in the woods.

Sophie wondered briefly if she had lost her mind — if the pregnancy had shaken up her mind so much that she had lost her marbles.

As Artemais gently took her hand and led her slowly back out of the woods, Sophie couldn't bear to keep her questions hidden.

"Are your brothers... Dom and Samuel... William...?"

Sophie smiled when Artemais released a breath he had been holding. She hadn't realized he had been silent too, letting her assimilate what he had shared.

"Yes. They are."

Nodding, she let him lead her a few more paces.

"What's it like?"

Sophie had been looking at the scenery, so when Artemais stopped she bumped into him. Warm hands reached out to hold her steady, embracing her in his heat. Turning into his chest, she nuzzled his neck a moment, enjoying the closeness she had with him. Sophie heard Artemais clear his throat. She nuzzled a bit more, teasingly this time when she found his cock hardening. She loved how he reacted so fiercely to her.

"It's painful, but not badly so. It's like coming home."

Sophie raised her head, worried.

"You feel more at home as a wolf?" She felt a bit relieved when he shook his head.

"That's not what I mean. When I change into a wolf, I feel free. I can smell the scents of the earth, run wild, be an animal. When I change into human form, I can feel my power, feel smarter, better. I'm at home in both bodies, and I'm blessed in that I feel relief and safety in both forms."

Sophie worried her lip.

"So how long do you run for? When you change into a

wolf? Will you leave me for days?"

Sophie refused to look at him, staring at the beauty of the Park; she tried to rationalize the fear and uncertainty gnawing at her gut. Could she cope with having her partner run wild for days at a time in wolf form? She wasn't sure.

Sophie felt her hand creep protectively over her stomach. Her child would be half werewolf. If for no other reason, she would make herself — teach herself — to deal with any of their idiosyncrasies, for the sake of her child. What she might not be willing to accept in a partner and lover, she would embrace and love in her child.

She felt Artemais' big hand tilt her chin upwards, so she had to look into his face.

"I'm Alpha, darling. I can chose when I change. I have to change on the night of the full moon, but I'm still me, still Artemais. I think slightly differently, but as a wolf or man, you are my mate. No other woman holds appeal for me. I doubt I could survive very long, and certainly not be content, without you by my side. On the night of the full moon, I'll run wild and free, yes. But I will *always* come back to you, to our son, to our home."

Sophie smiled and couldn't resist her teasing.

"Our daughter, you mean."

Artemais laughed, loud and long.

"If we are blessed with a daughter, I would love it. But genetics always seem to breed true for the Rutledges; I think you'll find our baby will be a boy. However, you can feel free to think otherwise. Either way, I simply must kiss you right now."

Sophie's breath caught as he dragged her even closer into his body. His hard muscles, his throbbing cock, his long, lean fingers as they traced a path down her spine. Everything he did set her body on fire. Pressing his lips to hers, she felt her doubts and fears melt away. Pressing back into him, she slid her tongue out and into his mouth, playing, dueling with his own.

When Artemais groaned, deep in his throat, Sophie felt an answering awareness in her body. She felt damp, her heartbeat accelerated, and her entire body strained forward for more attention.

"Sophie," Artemais started, obviously trying to keep a hold of his good intentions. Sophie nuzzled, then lightly bit his neck, sucking for a moment on the salty skin.

"Now, Artemais. I want you here, now. Please."

Sophie felt a rush of pleasure as Artemais lifted his head, looked wildly around them both, and then dragged her behind a particularly large tree.

"We really should…back to the house…" he panted, stringing kisses down her neck and unsnapping her jeans. Sophie grinned. It made her feel so much better to realize that it wasn't just her that felt so strongly affected by their attraction.

"Come on Artemais, live on the edge for a moment," she smiled softly, teasingly. The answering heat in his eyes, the fierce pressing of his hard cock showed he enjoyed her teasing.

"You want to live on the edge, huh, Soph? Let's try this then."

Sophie squeaked as Artemais turned her around and pressed her up against the large tree. He opened her jeans, then fumbled with his own, setting his large cock free. Sophie leaned back, ready for the lovely tight fit of Artemais' cock inside her, but when he kissed her again, then started playing with one breast and drawing damp patterns on her stomach, she shifted, being tickled.

"Artemais," she complained. When he only chuckled, and whispered "Patience" she knew she was in trouble.

He nipped and laved at her throat, and drove her body wild with his erotic patterns, his attention to her breasts. She could feel the heat radiating from his cock, as it pressed against her jeans and her panties, but he made no move to penetrate her.

Determined to tease him just as he teased her, she closed her hand around his cock in a tight fist, and pumped him once. Artemais pulled away from her slightly, his eyes flaring, his pupils dilating.

"Sophie," he growled warningly. She simply smiled back, trying to look innocent.

"Yes, Artemais?"

She pumped his cock again, squeezing her fist slightly as she reached the tip of his cock. She felt dampness as her finger swirled over his tip. An answering dampness wet her panties.

"Argh," he moaned, as Sophie pumped him a third time.

"I'm waiting Artemais," she chided gently, kissing under his ear and nipping the lobe gently.

"Fine," he growled, pulling her panties down so quickly she heard the delicate satin tear a bit. Her pussy finally exposed, the chill breeze sent goose bumps over her arms. In one heartbeat, Artemais covered her, shielding her from the breeze. She wound her arms around his neck, and tangled her legs in his.

"Shit, Soph. I feel like a schoolboy again."

Sophie smiled, and merely kissed him, drawing his tongue into her mouth as his long fingers explored her pussy. She was wet and impatient for him, but she could feel the massive effort he exerted over himself as he tried to delay their pleasure. When the pad of his finger grazed over her engorged clit, she cried out and arched into his hand.

Around and around, over and over he teased her clit, sending jolts of electricity through her system, driving her higher. When she could feel herself reaching that peak, she pulled him closer.

"Come with me," she panted. "Don't let me come alone!"

As Artemais gently held the head of his cock outside her pussy, Sophie swore she could feel its heat, feel him throbbing with the desire to enter her.

Then slowly, so very slowly she thought she would lose her mind, Artemais pushed himself into her. Inch by delicious inch he pressed. When he had a few inches inside her, he withdrew himself, tearing a cry from her.

"Please! Don't!"

When he chuckled and kissed her neck, Sophie clutched him with her inner muscles.

Yet again, he started pushing himself into her. First one inch, then another. When he lodged half inside her, he began to withdraw once again.

"No!" she cried, futilely trying to grasp him and pull him back inside her.

"Could you really leave me, love? Leave this?"

"No!" she panted, the husky timber of Artemais' voice turning her on even more than his physical actions.

"Our passion, our love for each other has already created one child inside you. I'm looking forward very much to creating another child, and then another. Do you want this Sophie?"

Sophie shrieked. When Artemais said *this* he pushed his entire length into her, filling her with his cock, with his words, with his heat and passion.

"Yes!" she cried out, uncaring of anyone hearing her screams, "I want it, Artemais. *Please!*"

With her screams of pleasure filling the woods, Artemais tilted her hips. At the angle he chose, he could slide even more deeply into her core.

The friction between her tight, clamping walls and the velvet skin of his cock, made her shudder. She wanted to scratch him, to pull him closer, to make him go faster. Instead, she threw her head back against the tree and moaned. Artemais groaned and ground his hips deeper into hers. As his thrusts became stronger, longer, she knew he lay on the brink of explosion, about to snap and lose his control.

With a low growl, Artemais seemingly read her mind and began to pump wildly into her. He buried his face into her hair, scenting her and wallowing in her soft hair.

Sophie's shirt and sweater stopped the rough abrasions of the bark from hurting her, and the pleasure from Artemais pumping into her and playing with her clit made all thoughts except that final peak fly from her head.

Suddenly, she saw stars, bright colors broke behind her closed eyes, and she couldn't stop the scream from leaving her throat. A second later, she felt Artemais thrust once more, even deeper inside her, groan and start to pulse. She felt his hot seed shoot up inside her, drench and fill her.

Feeling weak-kneed for the first time in her life, Sophie rested between the solid strength of her man and the tree. Feeling dazed, she felt unsure which one of them exactly held her up.

After a moment, when their breathing had returned to normal, she chuckled and kissed Artemais once more.

"Whoever said you don't know how to have fun?"

Grinning impishly at the slight flush that crept over his cheeks, Sophie watched as he hastily did his jeans up, and then returned a bit worriedly to her torn panties.

"I'm sorry, Sophie, I—"

"Don't worry about them. There's plenty more where they came from."

Zipping up her own jeans, kissing him again because she simply couldn't resist, she took his hand.

"Lead on MacDuff, your brothers are probably pacing, wondering what's happened to us."

Artemais turned to look at her, his eyes trailing hotly over her mussed hair and slight sexual glow. Sophie felt her face get a bit flushed and patted her curls in the vain attempt to make them sit back normally.

Artemais smiled a huge grin, pride and affection shining deeply in his blue eyes.

"I don't think my brothers will be wondering what we were doing at all, hon."

Slapping his shoulder, she tried to glare at him, but when he winked charmingly at her, she had to laugh.

"Fine, but I for one would like there to be a little mystery left. Let's get back to the house."

Wrapping his arm around her shoulders, Artemais led

her back to his home.

Chapter Sixteen

Dinner that night was a curious affair. William and Dominic grilled steaks, while she, Samuel and Artemais made salads. When they all were lazing about on the back patio, looking out into the woods, Sophie realized she found the lush green trees more magical, more special than she had ever known a forest to be. She had always loved nature, loved walking in parks, but somehow these woods seemed particularly special.

The brothers talked and laughed, ribbed and jested with one another. Dominic had flirted shamelessly with her, much to Artemais' disgust. In retaliation, Artemais had sat extremely close to her, one arm possessively draped over her shoulders, pulling her closer. Sophie could feel him vibrating with annoyance.

She had laughed at Dominic's overtures, knowing them for the playful flirting they were. He had winked at her cheekily when Artemais had been discussing something else with William, his face safely averted.

Artemais had finally simmered down, but only after she had whispered in his ear "Dominic is teasing you, hon. The more you rise to his flirting, the more he will do it. He doesn't mean anything by it, honest."

Artemais had finally worked it out, much to Sophie's relief, and wandered over to the grill to laugh and drink his beer with William and Samuel.

Dominic had pulled his chair up closer to hers, and

laughed hugely.

"I'm sorry, Soph. I hope you don't mind me playing with you. I just thought this is the perfect opportunity to show Brother Dear how to have a little fun and lighten up. He's always been the responsible one, never letting loose. I hope you can teach him to relax."

Sophie smiled back at Dominic.

"I find it hard to believe he's never had any fun. He seems to know all the rules to me."

Dominic had looked serious for a moment. Picking his words carefully, he toyed with a stray shoulder-length curl of his hair.

"It's not that he hasn't had fun, it's more that he's never *enjoyed* having fun. Never really cut loose and lost control, you know? He's always held himself in check, always remembered his responsibilities to the Pack and to us. He's effectively raised us from pups, and never let himself sit back and enjoy life. Do you see what I mean?"

Sophie smiled. It seemed incredible how much these brothers loved each other and how close they all were. She would have killed for even one sibling like this growing up. She had loved her Grandmother very, very much — but she had still been a very lonely little girl. She felt eternally grateful that her little girl would never know the sad loneliness she'd had while growing up. Her hand crept possessively and protectively over her still-flat abdomen in the age-old maternal gesture.

"Yeah. And now you think I'm here, there's someone who can finally convince Artemais to let loose and have a bit of fun? I thought *you* were the authority on types of fun around here, Dom. Has your reputation been blown all out of proportion due to your ego?"

Dominic smiled, brightening his whole face and bringing back that irresistible twinkle into his eyes, deepening his dimples. He let his head fall back as the huge bouts of laughter rolled from deep in his chest. Sophie could easily see the magnetic attraction this man could hold for any and all women.

"Of course my reputation hasn't been inflated. I've never needed to brag, the stories are only an inkling of what I can and will do for a lady."

Wiggling his eyebrows comically, he lent forward and whispered a raunchy, risqué suggestion in her ear. Blushing, she sat back and slapped his thigh, hard.

"I'm sorry I asked. No way are you getting anywhere near my children, male *or* female, until you're one hundred and ten and have a passel of your own children and grandchildren running around you keeping you tied down."

Laughing silently, lost in her mental picture of the huge old house overrun with dozens of children, some her own, some the children of Artemais' brothers, she didn't notice her hand creep protectively over her belly, over her growing little baby. Sophie also didn't notice Dominic eyeing her worriedly, lost as she was in her own romantic musings.

"Is my little nephew giving you problems?" he asked, concern clouding his features. Sophie blinked, startled. Looking down to her hand over her stomach for a moment, she looked back confused.

"No. Why?"

"Your hand is pressed into your stomach. Is he hurting?"

Sophie smiled.

"No. I was just thinking about how lucky my child would be with three uncles like you guys and such a great Daddy, even if you are all oversexed and overly hormonal. And this child could well be a girl. Why can't you boys accept that?"

Dominic grinned again, obviously relieved.

"All children in our line are boys. And I for one can't wait for the little man to grow up so I can show him a few things, teach him lessons I had to learn the hard way."

Sophie laughed. "I doubt you've *ever* had to learn anything the hard way, Dom. And if you want someone to mold into a little mini-you, you should go out and find your own partner and start having your own kids."

Dominic grinned mischievously.

"Now why would I want to tie myself down when you're here, already pregnant? I can simply live through your kids. You realize Artemais wants six, don't you?"

Sophie blinked, stunned.

"Six?"

Warm arms wrapped around her, along with Artemais' scent. He smelled of the forest, of wild green things and damp rain. She loved his smell, she realized, inhaling deeply.

"You'd think Dominic would let me drop my own bombs, wouldn't you?"

"But...*six*? Artemais, do you have any idea how much it will cost to feed, clothe and educate *SIX* children? I'm all for a large family, in fact, I insist on at least three. But I won't have more than four children. This may come as a shock to you, but I have it on the best of authority that it *hurts* to have children!"

"Oooh, the first lovers' quarrel," came an amused voice from behind her. Samuel nabbed a chair and swung it backwards, straddling it and facing Sophie and Artemais. Sophie simply glared at each brother in turn, finishing with William as he brought the steaks across the patio on plates.

"I don't see any of *you* offering to help bear these six mythical children."

Sophie had to grin at each happy male face. William tossed his long ponytail, taking his own seat.

"It's not our fault you women cornered the market on childbearing. You only have yourselves to blame for that."

Sophie rolled her eyes and took a delicious bite of the tender steak.

Laughing and jeering with the four men, Sophie felt lighter and happier than she had in years. She would never be lonely in this boisterous group. As all four men affectionately teased her, and insisted on the gender of her baby, Sophie relaxed and snuggled into Artemais' embrace.

She had no idea what the future held, but for now, her life felt full—complete. With a man obviously attracted to her, judging by the rocket he sported in his jeans, and enough laughter and love from these men to overflow a village, her world felt complete. She would never lack love and affection with these men, there was certainly enough for one woman and her baby.

Chapter Seventeen

Roland Matthews strained for a moment, then relaxed as the metallic *snap* of the wolf trap clicked into place. Gingerly inching back, he felt a strange mixture of guilt and hopeful satisfaction as he checked over the open trap.

As always whenever he wasn't sure if what he planned to do was right, he felt a momentary whisper of softness and the long-held memory of the scent of his mother brush over him.

Suddenly *really* unsure, Roland felt guilt assault him. For as long as he could remember, Roland had tried to become more like the memory he had of his mother, and not become the crazy husk of a man his father had been. He scrunched his face, trying to force the images of his early childhood from his mind.

As far back as he could remember his father had walked the razor edge of insanity. It wasn't until after he had died, being shot by a cop as he waved a huge cleaver around in a store, that the doctors and medical society had made the discovery of his brain literally being eaten away by syphilis.

His mother had been all the goodness and light, love and happiness in his life for his baby years. But she had deserted him; abandoned her crazed husband and her three-year-old son, and left him with a father who only knew brutal force and his own crazy, paranoid world. Even though he had only lived with his father for a little over the first thirteen years of his life, the man held a lasting impact on young Roland.

He had grown up perpetually fearful that he would share the same crazy fate of his father. In his late teens, as he had been passed around from foster home to foster home, he had always insisted on being tested, over and over, for syphilis. As his knowledge of the disease grew, and as he took utter control over his few sexual relationships, he had finally convinced himself he would not share his father's delusions.

Over the years, he had been incredibly cautious with his sexual partners. He hadn't been able to bear the thought of a child. Couldn't conceive of the responsibility of bringing a little baby into this world, a child who might be hurt and lost as he had been. As his mind drifted to picture his own tiny little baby... *NO!* He wouldn't think of him, of the woman whom he loved so dearly and, for her own safety, had left behind.

Forcing the mental pictures, the grief and huge aching hole of loss back into the darkest recesses of his mind, he reminded himself why he kept so far away from their perfection.

Losing his mother before his fourth birthday, and having police officers tell him before he turned fourteen of his father's death, it had almost been a relief to move into foster homes. Now he could keep his emotional distance and try to forge a life of his own, try to repent for his own sins and those of his father's.

His life wasn't a bed of roses, but it hadn't been complicated, until six years ago. At twenty-two, he had started having the dreams. The one thing his father's paranoia had focused on had been wolves. Wolves were dirty, wolves were the animals of the devil, wolves were the essence of evil. Over and over his father had raged and spat out obscenities about wolves, back as far as Roland could remember.

Roland had been worried, but not surprised that he had dreamed of wolves. But these dreams were fantastic. He was free, he could do anything, be anything. As his wolf-dream self, he could scent things and see things in an entirely different light.

Running wild through parklands, wallowing in scents of nature and of mankind. Roland loved his monthly dreams, but dreaded them too. He had decided that the guilt of all the wolves his father had killed had finally come down on him to haunt him. Through painful searching, he had managed to track down the start of his father's personal brand of madness against wolves, to here, Glacier National Park.

This place was where the madness had all started. Twenty-five years ago, as a three year old, Roland only had the vaguest memories of being in this area. Most of his memories from this era of his life were of his mother, and her softness.

As he thought and thought, he remembered a huge fight between his parents. Of his father raging against the wolves, in what would be the first of many tirades from his father, but the only one his mother witnessed.

Roland vaguely remembered his mother trying to placate his father. And the one and only time his father lashed out and hit his mother. He had been in a towering rage, his face flushed with anger, his eyes wild. His mother had stood back up, blood running down her face. She had been talking in that soft voice of hers, explaining he needed to "get used to it", but his father had walked out, slamming the door. Roland had crept up to his mother, watching her pack. She had cried, telling him she had something to do, but she would be back for him.

That had been the last time he had seen his mother. That night, his father had culled his first pack of wolves. Roland had no idea whether his father had sought out his mother, or whether she had simply never returned for her son, tainted with the blood of his father.

In the end, it had made little difference.

No records could be found of Janine Matthews, nor of Janine Simmonds, her maiden name.

Roland shook the old memories from him. He held a faint hope that if he could come back here — to the place where the nightmares started and the place he seemed to always roam to in his dreams — maybe he could exorcise them and move on with his life.

But he felt sick at the sight of the trap. He simply couldn't go through with it. Capturing a wolf wouldn't ease his guilt, nor ease the gnawing worry that he was loosing his mind like his father had before him.

As Roland hovered between carrying out his crazy scheme and halting before he truly hurt something, he felt a new sense of softness caress inside of him.

Helene.

Four years ago — during some of his most trying times — he had met the woman of his dreams, met Helene. She had been his one and only true love affair. She reminded him in so many ways of his mother. Her sweetness, her goodness, her caring. After six months of wallowing in her beauty, both within and without, he had tried to explain to her why he must leave.

He had been so fearful of turning her, of contaminating her with his tainted blood, with the bitterness and awful burden and wounds he carried around with him. Only with her had he felt hope, yet it would kill him to hurt or harm her in any way. She had professed to understand. During their time together he had told her more than he had any other human being. She understood. She didn't like his decision, nor agree with him, but as gentle and sweet as she was, she understood.

With tears in her eyes, she had watched him go. He had given her his pager number, so she could always contact him. The first time she had ever used it had been to give him the most important news he had ever received.

They had a son. She had called him Edward. The Guardian of Prosperity, the Guardian of the *Future*, Helene insisted. His future. *Their* future.

Roland had sworn there and then, both to himself and to Helene, he would heal himself, no matter what it required, and come make his home with her and their son. He called her weekly, just to talk to her and their child as he grew from a baby into a toddler.

He never quite admitted how desperately he missed her, though deep in his half-dead heart he felt she knew. He sent her all the money he could afford to give. He visited as often as he dared.

In his darkest, deepest part of his heart, he knew he loved them both. But he felt petrified it wouldn't be enough. What if he wasn't whole or healthy enough to make a go of his small family? The thought he might go mad like his father before him and hurt his Helene or son…the thought alone made him feel ill with worry.

As he felt Helene's goodness and light surround him, enfold him, Roland came back to the forest as if waking from another nightmare.

What the hell was he doing?

Standing up, and taking a small tree branch from the ground, he held it, about to set off the trap with the stick and remove it, when he saw a pale woman watching him from a couple of hundred feet away, through the woods.

She appeared washed out in the moonlight, short golden hair mussed, as if she had been roused from sleep. Not knowing if she had seen the trap or not, he called out to her, wanting to warn her not to come too near.

"Hey!"

Startled, she turned and began to flee.

"Hey!" he called out a second time, cursing under his breath.

Roland quickly stabbed the branch into the trap, setting it off so no animals would be caught in it. Satisfied when he heard the sickening *snap*, he raced after the woman. He didn't know who she was or what she wanted, but he didn't want her reporting him when nothing had happened. His deep-seated fear of the police had his gut clenching in worry.

He had never really gotten over his fear of police. Spending time in lock-up, trying to explain his crazy actions and insane reasonings, all the while petrified of the cops certainly came high on his list of things *not* to have happen.

Chapter Eighteen

Sophie had woken in the middle of the night, disorientated for a moment. She felt the hard press of a masculine body next to hers; one leg wrapped over her hips, and felt a second of panic.

The previous day washed over her as she remembered.

Artemais.

After dinner, they had all played poker for an hour. Sophie had won the entire pot, having never mentioned that her grandmother, rather than playing the mandatory old-lady bingo, had been a card shark. She had taught her granddaughter to play poker against the best. Sophie had won game after game, gleefully ripping off all four brothers, much to their groans of disgust.

Artemais had finally thrown his cards onto the table in exasperation, hauled Sophie out of her seat and thrown her over his shoulder.

"I'm taking her to bed. My ego won't stand for any more beating tonight. I'm sure we'll get our revenge tomorrow night. 'Night guys."

Rowdy laughter and catcalls followed them out from the kitchen, as Artemais carried her up to his room. Making passionate love to her, over and over, she had finally fallen into an exhausted sleep.

But something had woken her up, and Sophie couldn't put her finger on it.

Easing herself out from under Artemais' splayed body; she shivered, pulled on a pair of jeans and a sweater and opened the window. Staring out into the moonlit night, she intuitively knew she needed to go for a walk. Silently pulling on socks and running shoes, she crept out of the house, into the backyard and out into the woods.

Something about these woods drew her. She had no idea where the drawing feeling came from, but she felt as if she were trapped in a book from her childhood. Magical trees, forests, whimsical creatures, and werewolves. Her brain whirled with activity, as she sucked in deep lungful of the fresh night air. Cracking twigs as she wandered around the woods, she circled a perimeter around the back of the house, not wanting to move too deeply in case she got lost.

Suddenly, she heard a loud metallic *snap*. The knowledge that she wasn't alone in these woods had a jarring effect on Sophie. Wishing she had woken up Artemais for her midnight stroll, she froze, glancing around her, looking for whomever she could hear near her.

Even though it was dark, the moonlight cast a glow around the forest, and Sophie had no trouble seeing the surrounding area. Finally seeing the figure of a man as he stood up from the ground, Sophie crept forwards, wondering what he was doing. He wore faded jeans and a woolen sweater, so she couldn't place him as a park ranger. She couldn't think of a reason for anyone else to be in the area.

Halting once she had him clearly in view, Sophie looked around the strange man, trying to figure out what he was doing.

Then she saw the huge trap.

Large and silver, it glinted menacingly in the moonlight. Scared, Sophie felt sick for a moment, worried she would puke there and then. The thought of any helpless creature, let alone any of the wild wolves in the park getting caught in the trap made Sophie feel physically ill.

Just when she had decided to turn around and go back to collect Artemais, the man picked up a huge fallen branch, and he looked right up to her.

"Hey!" he called out.

Panic welled in her, she couldn't think or breathe. Sophie simply reacted, turned and fled.

"Hey!" the man called again. There was another, much louder, sickening *snap* and then twigs snapping as the man undoubtedly started to follow her. Adrenaline rushing into her system, Sophie ran faster, twigs and branches catching on her arms and face, scratching her and slowing her down.

Determined not to squeal or shriek like a girl, Sophie concentrated simply on running. Large, heavy footfalls fell behind her, and Sophie could hear the man chasing after her, spurring her into a faster flight.

Panting, Sophie had no idea where she was anymore, or which direction the house lay. After what felt like eons, but might have been a minute or two, a heavy arm clasped her shoulder, pulling her to a stop.

"Hey!" the man panted, "I'm not going to hurt you. I just want to explain."

"There's really not much to explain. Honest. Just let me go," she replied, gulping in air.

The man held onto her shoulder, hard, but not causing her any pain. He awkwardly ran his other hand through his hair, seemingly searching for words.

"Look, I'm here to find some answers. I thought that would work, but it won't. I set off the trap; I'll go back and get it. I was going to dismantle it before I saw you anyway."

Sophie took another look at this man. Something seemed strange about him. He looked tense, not just that guilty-been-caught-doing-something-naughty, tense, but also an underlying anxiety or burden. Something really seemed to be eating away at this man.

Under different circumstances, Sophie would have felt her heart go out to this man. She might have tried to soothe him, calm his fears. But it was dark, and she felt scared and alone. While she felt a pang of pity for this guy and whatever his problems were, her mind kept racing, reminding her she needed to get back to the house. That and she obviously still had too much adrenaline pumping through her system from their chase and flight.

Uncertain how to move on from here, Sophie tried to placate him.

"Look, I was just going for a walk. I didn't mean to pry. I'm sure you'll take that trap back. I just want to go now." Sophie carefully, slowly, stepped out from under his grip. "I hope you find what you're looking for." Taking a step back, then another, Sophie collided into a hard, masculine body.

Shrieking, she jumped back, turning around.

William stood there, half hidden in the darkness cast by a tree. He didn't look very pleased. Reaching out, he drew Sophie protectively under his shoulder.

"Sophie. You'll catch a chill. Who's your friend?"

Sophie grinned. William fairly vibrated with

protectiveness. It felt kind of cute in an annoying way.

"I don't know William, why don't you ask him yourself? I didn't get around to introducing myself."

The man squinted up at William, obviously more ill at ease than before.

"I'm Roland Matthews." Holding his hand out to William, he waited a moment for William to take his hand and shake it. William's body froze a little as he clasped Roland's hand. If Sophie weren't being held so close to him, she wouldn't have noticed. William's nostrils flared for a moment, as he inhaled deeply.

"Roland. What exactly are you looking for?" he asked, obviously having overheard the end of their conversation.

Roland fidgeted.

"I'm not sure. Look, I need to go pick up that trap. I should be able to find it, then I'd better head on out."

"Maybe we should catch up. I might be able to help you. I've lived in this area all my life," William offered, voice casually smooth, but steel obviously underlying his offer.

Roland blinked, obviously hearing the steel. "Uh. Sure. Thanks," he mumbled.

"Where are you staying? I can come over tomorrow morning sometime to start your search," William pressed.

"I'm in the local motel. Just down in the village a few miles out." He sighed, resigned.

"Until tomorrow then. Come on Sophie. Let's get you warm."

Steering Sophie as if she were a sheep, William turned them both around and headed back towards where she assumed the house stood.

Once they were out of earshot, Sophie stepped out from under his shoulder, and berated him.

"What the hell did you think you were doing, William? I was just out for a stroll—" Sophie didn't even get to finish her lecture before William set in.

"What the hell did you think *you* were doing? These woods aren't safe for you to walk alone in at night! Why isn't Art with you? I should turn you over my knee!"

Sophie gasped.

"You wouldn't dare! Art—Artemais was asleep and I'm a big girl. I can go walking at night alone if I want to! Neither of you are my keeper and I'm not locked up in some jail cell!"

William leaned closer, pulling her to a halt and leaning right into her face.

"Don't tempt me, Sophie dear. You know I'm a cop, one of the very few all the way out here. If I think locking you up is best for your own protection, I damn well will. That man is strange, and you should be thanking your lucky stars I heard you leave the house and decided to follow you."

"Follow me! Why—" Sophie spluttered and fairly choked on her words of annoyance, "How dare you—?" before she could finish her righteous rant, something else William just said hit her.

"Strange? Strange how, William? What did you pick up on when you shook his hand?"

William grabbed her arm and started striding back to the house. He finally answered as it came into view.

"That man is a werewolf. I just don't think he knows it, or won't admit it yet. I'm not sure. He smells...strange, like a werewolf, but also like a human. I don't really understand. All I know is he's strange, and you're not to go near him again. Understand?"

Sophie sniffed, trying to look disdainful as she scurried to keep up with his long strides.

"I don't take orders from you or any man, William," she stated haughtily.

"We'll see." He muttered ominously.

* * * * *

"*You did what?*" Artemais shouted, still mussed and half-asleep. Throwing back the comforter and striding forward, gloriously naked, Sophie averted her eyes, suddenly a little less confidant. William stood at the door, arms crossed over his chest. Sophie would bet money he would have smirked if this had been any other circumstance. She blushed at Artemais' nudity—even if neither he nor William seemed to care about it.

"William, tell me this is some sort of joke to piss me off." Without even waiting for William's confirmation, he turned back to Sophie.

"You can't just go wandering off at night around here. Sweet Jesus, this isn't a normal city park where the most dangerous animals are sparrows!" Running an agitated hand through his hair, mussing it further, Artemais seemed at a loss for words.

Sophie crossed her hands protectively across her chest. She had asked William to be quiet as she returned to Artemais' room. He had said it wouldn't make a difference—that Artemais would wake up as she returned anyway. But she hadn't believed him. If she had she would have spent the night downstairs on the couch. *Next time she would*, she decided.

"Come on Artemais, you'd think I'd been caught stealing from the secret chocolate stash, from the way you're acting. All I did was take a little walk for some fresh air."

Artemais took a step further, obviously still angry.

"You're more than welcome to any and all the chocolate in the house, Sophie, you know that. But for heaven's sake, you can't just go wandering off in the middle of the night!"

Sophie sighed. They were both tired and disjointed — obviously not the best time to start a fight.

"Look," she soothed, going up to her agitated lover and wrapping her arms around his neck. "Nothing happened. I'm fine. I needed a bit of fresh air and simply wanted to go for a walk. I bumped into some guy called Roland purely by accident. I bet if I'd done this on any other night nothing at all would have happened. Can we go back to sleep now, please?"

Artemais exchanged a look with William. The two men almost seemed to communicate without speaking. William finally nodded, grinning. Giving Sophie a chaste kiss on her cheek, he wished her a good night, and left the bedroom, softly closing the door behind him.

"Now, Sophie," Artemais started, but she cut him off.

"You can vent at me tomorrow Artemais. I'm tired, let's just go to sleep." As she started casually stripping her clothes off, Artemais drew in a ragged breath, and nodded.

"Tomorrow," he promised, climbing back into the

large bed.

As he drew her down, naked and pliant into his arms, he kissed her softly, gently.

Sophie opened her mouth, letting her tongue clash with his and join the mini-mating dance. Artemais groaned and deepened his tongue's penetration. Rolling her over, so his long body totally covered her own, he nudged her legs apart with his thigh.

"I need you," he whispered huskily. "When I woke up and saw you enter the room, realized you'd gone out without me, I felt so scared. Anything could have happened to you, to our baby..."

"Shh," Sophie comforted him. "I'm here. I promise I'll wake you up next time."

Artemais groaned, kissed her again and fondled one nipple, feeling it bud in his palm. Sophie arched up into him, greedy for more attention.

"Now, Artemais," she whispered heatedly in his ear. "I want you. Hard and hot. Right now."

Artemais moved his hand down from her nipple, down into her curls. Feeling her wet and warm, just for him, he couldn't wait a second longer. Placing his rigid cock outside her entrance, he paused for a second, making her squirm with anticipation. Without preliminaries, he thrust into her with one stroke.

Sophie cried out, the pleasure exquisite. She arched up into Artemais' embrace, both his intimate one and his hot, embracing body. Scratching his back, marking him with her nails, she gutturally begged him for more. Artemais felt a surge of pride, of possession. This woman was his. She didn't realize it, but she was marking him as hers, as he intended to mark her.

Bending low, thrusting his fiercely aroused cock deeper and deeper into her, he bit the spot just above her collarbone. Gently, he sucked on the skin, creating a warm tingle. Marking the skin in the non-visible, permanent manner of his people. Artemais branded Sophie as his alone and thus sealed both their fates.

For better or worse, he had branded her as his. Even as the love bite faded, his essence, his scent would remain on her, warning all others of his kind away from her.

As Sophie arched up, again and again, coming and creaming all over his heavy cock, he let himself go and climaxed himself. Shooting his seed deep into her body, he collapsed over her, sated and happy.

She snuggled into him, rested and warm, quickly falling asleep. Artemais lay quiet for a moment, knowing there was more to the story that William hadn't told him, but hadn't wanted to tell him with Sophie listening in. He had that feeling deep in his gut that something strange was afoot, and he'd have to fix it.

Sighing, he curved his body protectively over Sophie's, wrapping his arms and legs into a tangled mess around her. No way was she getting up for any more midnight strolls again.

He had learned his lessons the first time.

Chapter Nineteen

Sophie came down the stairs and entered the kitchen, grumpy as always in the mornings.

Artemais had already gone down before her, calling out his intentions so she could hear him over the shower spray. One of Sophie's few indulgences, other than chocolate and ice cream, were always long, hot showers. It was the only thing in the morning that even held the possibility of rousing her from her bed. She hated not being able to drink coffee.

She hated mornings, and she hated chirpy people who always seemed to expect others to be bright and cheery in the morning.

Glancing around grumpily at the four studly men lounging in the kitchen, buttering toast, scrambling eggs, and pouring percolated coffee, she pulled out a chair and settled herself down, rubbing blearily at her eyes.

"Good morning, sweetheart," Artemais started, far too chirpily. He *knew* she hated the morning. It had taken him considerable effort and a lot of bribery to get her up this morning. "Would you like some eggs, or toast, or maybe some cold cereal?"

Sophie stuck her tongue out at him.

"Just some juice thanks. I'm not hungry. It's too early to eat just yet."

William sat down next to her, his mug filled with coffee and a huge plate piled high with toast. Grinning at her, he took a healthy swallow of the coffee and offered her some toast.

"Eat up kid. You're packing it in for two now."

Before Sophie could think of a witty comeback, William froze, looked at her carefully, and inhaled deeply. Sophie fought a smile at the thought that a few days ago this would have freaked her out. At some time over the last forty-eight hours she had come to regard these men as her family.

William stared at her collarbone, primly covered with her sweater against the morning chill. Sophie felt herself blush. *He can't see the hickey*, she reminded herself. But with the strange reaction he showed, then the huge bouts of laughter, as he threw his head back and let loose with his chuckles, Sophie had the uneasy sensation that there was a huge joke going around she wasn't privy to.

"Well done, brother. About time, even if I do say so myself."

"What?" Sophie grumped hostilely. "What are you laughing over?"

Wondering about the huge ruckus, both Samuel and Dominic left their bickering over the skillet over whether to cook all six strips of bacon, or only four strips, to come over and see what had their brother laughing so loudly. Standing on either side of her, they also froze, inhaling deeply. Sophie decided enough was enough. She loved these guys, but she felt sick and tired of them sniffing around her like a bunch of dogs around a tasty bone.

"Stop it you two!" she grumped, crossing her arms over her chest for protection. Glaring at Artemais, who wore a huge toothy grin and a smug look of male satisfaction, she imagined for one wonderful moment how he would look while she choked him.

"Make them stop, Artemais."

Snapping back to reality, Samuel patted her on the back while Dominic punched Artemais with brotherly affection on his arm. Both men congratulated him and complemented him on his prowess.

Not liking the undertones, nor her non-understanding of the joke, Sophie stood up to make her own damn breakfast.

"Would anyone like pancakes?" she sweetly asked, hoping to change the topic of conversation onto more normal footing.

"Oh man," complained William, "I can't do justice to those and the toast. Tomorrow?" he begged, eyes wide. Sophie sighed, and helped herself to Dominic's almost-burning scrambled eggs and bacon.

Sophie ate and drank her fresh orange juice, slowly waking up and becoming her usual, happy self. When Samuel had gently and oh-so-carefully asked her about morning sickness and if that were the cause of her grumpiness, she had smiled, winking at Artemais.

"It doesn't appear that I get morning sickness, Sam. I am always this grumpy in the morning." Laughing at his confused expression, she had continued, "I seem to get afternoon sickness. I'm not a morning person, and neither is my child apparently."

After doing justice to the food, and feeling much better for having something solid in her stomach, Sophie asked Artemais if he could show her around the park and little village nearby.

"Actually Soph," Artemais cleared his throat, looking warily at her, "I was hoping you could do a bit of shopping yourself this morning. I'll be more than happy to show you around the park and woods later this afternoon, after lunch. But I have…er…business…to do this morning."

Sophie looked carefully at her lover. "Business," she stated, tasting the word in her mouth. Something was obviously up, but what? Artemais flinched at that single word she uttered, but continued with his explanations anyway.

"Yes. Business. You know about the security company. Our main offices are in town, but I can take care of most aspects of it here from home. The wonders of phone, fax and the internet." He smiled at her, but Sophie noticed it wasn't his normal smile, it seemed strained and more than a bit forced.

Sophie looked around the table at the rest of his brothers. They all looked at her, with differing levels of expectation. Dominic seemed eager and even as if he looked forward to her exploding. William looked pensive, as if he didn't agree with Artemais. Samuel grinned cheekily at her, obviously happy with any sort of reaction she gave him.

"Let me get this straight. You want me to go to that tiny village a couple of miles back down the road, and spend the morning shopping. While you do…" Sophie dragged out the word, obvious disbelief in her voice, "…business."

Artemais grinned, obviously not understanding her skepticism and disbelief.

"Sure thing, sweetie. Here's my card."

Reaching into his back pocket for his wallet, he pulled out a gold card and pressed it into her hands.

Sophie realized Artemais was getting rid of her, and panic welled for a moment. It abated the moment inspiration struck.

"William is going to tell you whatever was bothering him last night about that man, isn't he?"

She smiled at the shock her words created in the room. Dominic and Samuel's stupid, cheesy grins had been replaced by an annoyingly masculine concern.

"Man?"

"What man?"

"Wills, what's been happening?"

Sophie grinned, pocketed the gold card and exacted her revenge while stealing the Jeep keys from the hook by the door.

"Oh, I went for a walk alone in the woods last night," she paused for a split second while Dominic and Samuel uttered cries, their jaws slackening in shock. "I came across a man setting up some sort of wolf or bear trap thing. I got scared and ran, and he caught up to me and explained he was looking for some answers and had decided not to do what he planned after all. Then William came out of nowhere, intending on 'rescuing' me, and dragged me back to the house. Did I miss anything?"

Artemais simmered, shaking his head mutely.

"So now I get to go play little woman and spend your money carelessly while you and your *men* get to plot and plan, hmmm? Well sure, I can spend money better than any woman. I'll be back around lunchtime, *darling*."

With that she tossed the keys in the air, caught them, snagged her purse, and headed out the back door towards the Jeep. Hearing raised male voices coming from the kitchen, Sophie grinned and started the car. She'd see what sort of shopping the village offered, and afterwards she could relax in a café or something and plot *her* revenge.

Damn him anyway for trying to keep her out of the loop. She had known William found something out, maybe recognized the man from somewhere, but she didn't know how or when. Never mind, she could ponder it as she had a hot chocolate. Chocolate always made everything better, even if she was supposed to avoid caffeine right now.

Chapter Twenty

Artemais watched Sophie through the kitchen window as she walked toward the Jeep. With her well-worn jeans hugging her curvy ass and the sexy swing in her step, even upset as he felt, he wanted her badly.

Filtering out his brothers' raised voices, he pondered the complexities of his feelings as she started the Jeep and made a three-point turn that curdled his blood. Wincing at how close she came to the big old elm trees lining the gravel driveway, and then at the rocks that spewed forth under the wheels as she accelerated too hard, Artemais thanked the gods that he wasn't in the passenger seat next to her, and prayed for her safety on the small dirt roads.

Once he could no longer see her, he turned back to his brothers, all of whom were staring at him like he had recently arrived from an alien planet.

"Since when have women become so damned complicated?" he groused.

Three big, cheesy grins faced him over the table.

"Well, it could have something to do with your mate having a mind of her own, not being like those brainless bimbos you used to hang out with," Samuel started. "What do you think Dom?"

"Gotta agree with you bro, Soph is a firecracker all right. Bet she'll put a lovely dent in that credit rating of yours, huh?"

Artemais groaned and sunk his head in to his hands.

He was doomed. Between his brothers' teasing and Sophie's antics—how could she have gone walking in the woods in the middle of the night?—he knew he would go gray, lose all his hair, and age a century in the next decade. When William added his two cents, he thought he would bring his breakfast back up again.

"Of course, it doesn't help that you love her to distraction, and she's pregnant with your baby and has no idea of her own safety."

"Oh, shit," Artemais cursed, rushing over to the sink to rinse his face and wrists in cold water as he broke out into a sweat. Even the *thought* of Sophie in danger, of not understanding how precious she and their baby were, brought a cold sweat to his brow and made his stomach clench menacingly.

All three of his brothers surrounded him, hovering like nursemaids. Artemais grabbed control of himself, stood up and went back to his seat.

"Okay, enough of this. Sophie is just going down to the village to spend my money and she'll be fine. No one there will hurt her—in fact some of the Pack will probably be highly amused at my mark on her. William, what was with this guy in the park last night? What happened?"

Briefly, William explained how he had woken up last night to the creak of floorboards as Sophie had crept out, how she had wandered aimlessly in the forest, breathing in the night air. He described in as much detail as possible the man, whom he had seen long before Sophie had, and the wolf trap he had set. How Roland had paused, then picked up the stick and Sophie had finally seen him, panicked, and run off.

"He called himself Roland Matthews, and said he was

born in this area. He didn't seem to be lying. He smelled of human as well as werewolf—but it seemed as if he hid his wolf side. I've never smelt anything like him, I was toying with the idea that he hadn't changed yet."

"Matthews…" mused Artemais as his brothers tossed around ideas and suggestions. Knowing his grandfather was out on a solitary hiking expedition, he wondered who would be next best to call for information.

Lifting up the phone, he dialed a well-known number. Clicking his fingers to get the guy's attention for silence, he greeted the man on the other end of the phone.

"Hey there, Old Tom. Artemais here. How are you doing?"

Waiting a few moments for the older man to list out his grumbles and complaints, Artemais finally got back on track.

"Matthews, Roland being the son, does the name ring any bells? He's what, Will? Mid-twenties?" waiting for William's nod, he continued, "Around his mid-twenties, says he grew up here. Any connection to someone in the Pack?"

"*Matthews hmm?*" the old voice on the other end mused. "*Been a while since I've heard that name. That pretty young girl, Janine, married a Matthews. They had a young boy, too, if memory serves. I do believe Janine died in the culling. Father and son disappeared soon after. I can check with Mona and see if anything else crops up, as long as she's having a good day. I wasn't around that month — off courting the Mrs.*"

"That's fine. Thanks Old Tom, we can go down to Mona's today, check on her and see how she is. So it's likely the son could have the blood, huh?"

"Quite likely, son. He back in town, is he?"

"Seems to be, Tom. Thanks again for the help."

Exchanging pleasantries, Artemais hung up and filled his brothers in. They talked through their various ideas and solutions. Around eleven, Artemais finally declared it time to do something.

"Let's go have a chat with him, if for nothing else to press home that traps are not the answer to any of his problems. Sophie has the Jeep, let's take your truck, William."

They headed out, still arguing over what to tell young Roland.

Chapter Twenty-One

Sophie took the last bite of her carrot cake with cream cheese frosting and chocolate drizzle, and sat back, a satisfied smile on her face and hand over her stomach. She pondered for a moment the wisdom of ordering a second slice, but decided against it when she thought of the waitress' knowing smirk when she had requested chocolate topping to be drizzled over her slice of cake.

"Ah, expecting Artemais' baby, huh? You must be the fiancée then."

Sophie had blinked; trying to understand the huge leap the woman had taken. "What on earth makes you say that?"

The waitress had waved the Gold Card about, clearly excited.

"I thought not even the devil himself could have pried Artemais' Gold Card out of his dead hands. Calls it his company's security. I knew you were someone important when you came in with it, but after that strange request, you simply have to be knocked up."

Sophie had bristled, "I'll have you know that chocolate topping drizzled over cake is a favorite dessert for me. I'll also have a hot chocolate with extra whipped cream please." Looking haughty and as offended as she could — she had never in her life put topping on her cake, it had simply been a whim — Sophie relaxed once the waitress had shrugged and taken her order. Sitting at the window looking out at the main street of the village, Sophie grimaced.

His company's security? she worried.

She felt so grateful now that she had calmed down on the short drive down the dirt track. The "village" consisted of a small grocery store, small motel, a library—which wouldn't open until noon—a few small craft and toy stores, and one women's clothes store.

Entering it, she had discovered it doubled as a lingerie store and adult bookstore. Buying herself a lacy camisole, Sophie had pored over the sexy lingerie. It had been ages since she had splurged on herself, so she bought some sexy bra and panty sets. Unearthing a pair of blue lacy crotchless panties in the bargain bin, Sophie had been curious.

She had never worn a pair of crotchless panties before, but she assured herself that now was a perfectly good time to start. She had tried them on in the miniscule fitting room, pleased to find they fitted her comfortably. They were a little drafty compared to her ordinary silk and lace panties, but one had to make sacrifices in the name of fashion. Thinking of a few naughty ways to let Artemais find her in these, she had discreetly added them to her basket, and continued searching the back of the store.

Sophie found to her delight a black garter belt with matching suspenders and black lace thigh-highs. Scrounging around, she found a black and red patterned bustier to finish the ensemble. Really into her spending groove, Sophie wandered around, touching and smelling things, until she came across a pair of fur-lined handcuffs.

Remembering the naughty words Dominic had whispered into her ear at dinner last night, she felt herself smirk, wondering if she could possibly get away with restraining Artemais like this.

Having pored through everything the more adult aspect of the shop held, Sophie returned to the simple lingerie again and added three silky thongs just for fun.

Mentally trying to tally her expenditures, Sophie had decided her revenge on Artemais would be almost over before it began. Adding a tube of lavender and rose scented massage oil to the basket on a whim; she walked bravely over to the checkout.

The woman had looked oddly at her for a moment, sniffed discretely, and grinned widely at Artemais' Gold Card. She had wrapped the lingerie discreetly in thin tissue paper, placed the handcuffs in a smaller bag, and added everything into one shopping bag, with the camisole on top to cover the other purchases.

"Have a wonderful day, Miss," the sales girl had grinned, winking knowingly.

Now knowing that the sales clerk had probably worked out who she was, Sophie wondered if *everyone* here became a werewolf over the full moon. Knowing it unlikely, Sophie had sipped her chocolate, eating the cream with a spoon, and tried not to think of her home and little apartment.

When the bell above the café door tinkled, she had looked up, curious.

It was Roland. He caught sight of her, smiled shyly, and came over.

"May I join you?" he asked politely.

Nodding, Sophie indicated the seat next to her.

"What can I help you with?" she asked, curious. Sophie could feel Roland's indecision as he sat down.

"You can accept my apologies, for one. I am so sorry if I scared you last night. I believe I was born here, but my father moved us after my mother abandoned us when I was only three. A couple of months ago...circumstances arose and I decided to come back and try to sort some things out. I guess I'm a little more screwed up by it all than I originally thought. I really am sorry if I upset or scared you."

Sophie felt her anger at Roland melt. Resting a hand casually on his arm, she reassured him.

"That's okay, but hurting other animals and people isn't going to make you feel any better. You need to work out whatever is bugging you, and accept it. Then you can move on and find some happiness."

Before she could continue, the waitress had bumped into her, dislodging her hand and startling her.

"Would you like to order, sir?" she said briskly and a little rudely. "We have a number of specials on today. The soup will be ready soon. It's vegetable..."

Sophie tuned out the waitress as she wondered why she had not only cut off their conversation, but literally stood in front of her, totally cutting her out of Roland's line of sight. She wasn't annoyed at the waitress' interference, but she certainly felt confused.

When the door jangled again, cutting into her thoughts, Sophie saw a very angry-looking Artemais storming through the door. She smiled, welcoming the distraction to her thoughts, until he reached her side and wrapped a very strong, very possessive arm around her shoulders, crushing her close to his warm body.

Sophie felt Samuel, William and Dominic flanking Artemais, but squashed into his body as she was, she couldn't see them, merely feel their heavy presence around her and Artemais.

"Roland." Artemais growled. "What the hell are you doing here with my woman?"

Sophie felt a moment of panic, and then outrage flooded her.

"Artemais!" she hissed, "Don't you dare embarrass me. I was simply sitting here drinking hot chocolate and he came in to apologize."

Roland looked at the four stormy faces, and smiled uncertainly.

"She's right. I came in for some late brunch, and saw her here. I had already planned on dropping by your place later this afternoon anyway and apologizing, but since I already saw her here…" he trailed off, looking back at the waitress.

"The chef's burger and coffee will do fine, thank you, ma'am."

The waitress took one look at the Rutledge brothers and scurried off into the kitchen. Artemais fairly growled with anger, his brothers simply standing by him, waiting for him to calm down and make a decision. Sophie noticed the chef, a tall, fat, balding man with a greasy apron come out of the kitchen, obviously angry at the possibility of a brawl in his café.

Deciding the levels of testosterone in the room were way too high, Sophie wrapped an arm around Artemais' neck. Bringing his head down, so she could whisper in his ear, she softly said, "I went shopping in the ladies' store, Art." As he froze, obviously his full attention now tuned in to her, she continued the light, breathy naughty words as they simply poured from her soul. "Did you know there's an adult part to the shop in the back? Well, they had these tiny, blue lace, crotchless panties. Seeing as I had *your* Gold Card with me, I thought I'd put some of your money to good use. There's nothing better than a pair of tiny, skimpy lace with an oh-so-large hole right where my slit can be accessible just for you."

As Artemais started breathing heavily, his pupils dilating and his breath choking in his lungs, Sophie heard what sounded definitely like a snort coming from Dominic's mouth. Glaring at him and dragging Artemais even closer, whispering softer, she finished with, "The blue is the same bedroom blue of your eyes. I bought them just with you in mind. Can we go home now? They're in the bag under the table by my chair. I'm feeling a little...hot, darling."

Artemais stood up straight, glared at Roland for a moment and then pointed one long finger at him.

"Don't you leave town. I'll come speak to you later this afternoon." As he glanced once more at Sophie, he amended, "Or maybe closer to dinnertime."

Picking up the small bag Sophie had indicated under the table, he grabbed Sophie's hand and hauled her to the door. Snickering, Sophie followed, waving at the chef and waitress and jingling the keys to the Jeep.

When reminded to buckle up, Artemais simply snapped, "Drive," and she laughed outright. He could be such a straight-laced stick in the mud, but Sophie figured she almost had hang of him.

This would certainly be fun.

Chapter Twenty-Two

Artemais tried his best not to howl in sexual frustration. Sophie had turned him into a frustrated, muddled idiot of a sexual slave. When he had caught sight of her talking to that man, her hand lightly resting on his arm, her face so very serious, he had wanted to rend and tear something, to kill anything that came into his path.

As he had halted his progress, and turned to storm into the small café, he had seen Rita cut between the two, and Sophie had looked so confused he had realized she hadn't had any sort of sexual meaning to her light touch.

That knowledge had eased his hurt, but hadn't tempered his anger any. She was *his*, they were as good as mated. He hadn't had time to utter any of the pretty words she obviously expected, but still, he couldn't believe the jealousy and possessiveness coursing through him.

He decided then and there to marry her in a hurry — as soon as possible in fact. When she had pulled him close, trying to distract him, and started whispering those naughty, heated things, his mind had scattered and only her scent, her breath, her words had mattered. Everything else in the world had faded away, until only Sophie's softness, and her heated words, the images they brought to him, had held him.

Looking down to the plain plastic bag sitting in his lap, he threw a heated glance over to her.

"So what else is in this bag, or were you simply

teasing me?"

As Sophie blushed, he knew she hadn't lied about the panties. Opening the bag eagerly, he saw the dark purple, skimpy lacy camisole. Pulling it out, he admired it.

"Very nice, but not quite what I was looking for."

Before he could dig deeper, Sophie had reached across him and snatched the bag out of his lap and shoved it under her seat.

"You can't look just yet. Some of that is a surprise. Leave a girl a few secrets, would you?"

Grinning deeply, he leered, pressing close to her shoulder.

"Aw, come on, darling. You've worked me up into a frenzy, just like you wanted. You're not going to leave me hanging now, are you?"

At the potent, heated look she gave him, he nearly swallowed his tongue. She definitely wasn't planning on leaving him hanging long, if her glance had anything to do with her feelings.

The dirt and gravel spewed everywhere as she turned into their driveway in third gear. Artemais held onto the side of the door, swearing to always wear his seatbelt while Sophie sat behind the wheel. As she slammed on the brakes and pulled the parking brake on, Artemais opened the door carefully.

Sophie ran ahead of him, laughing and taunting him.

"Catch me if you can, big boy, or if you dare!"

He watched her leap up the front stairs and throw open the door, leaving it open as she ran in the direction of the stairs up to his rooms.

Artemais followed at a more sedate pace. He wanted

to give Sophie just enough time to change into those panties. Some things were definitely worth a bit of patience. Getting a glass of water from the kitchen tap, and taking his time walking up the stairs, Artemais felt the excitement build up in him.

As he paused in front of his own bedroom door, he raised his hand and knocked briskly.

"Who is it?" came the sultry reply.

"It's me," he stated, slightly impatiently. He had merely knocked to warn her of his arrival, not to be polite.

The door opened a crack, and Sophie's blonde curls, mussed adorably, peered through the crack, her gray eyes sparkling with mischievousness.

"I know a few 'me's. Which one are you?" she pressed, the mirth in her eyes plain for him to see.

Artemais decided there and then to play this game of hers out to the end. He had a lot of experience winning his games.

Pushing the door open gently, he was careful not to exert enough force to hurt her, but enough to have her backing up to let him in.

"I," he said softly, "am your Lord and Master."

Sophie's eyes twinkled so much he knew she had to be repressing her laughter.

"Oh really?" she stepped back to allow him into the room, and after he closed the door behind him and faced her he took a deep breath. Which promptly caught in his throat.

She wore a royal blue lace bra, which did nothing to hide her soft brown nipples and pale creamy complexion. Her lovely full breasts—which were already a mouthful for him—rose up, high and firm, taunting him. With a matching blue short pleated skirt, she looked as if she were getting dressed. As she reached over onto his bed to pick up a dark cream silk business shirt, and began to put it on, he held out an arm to stop her.

"What do you think you're doing?"

"Getting ready. You said we were going out remember?"

Artemais had never felt so off-kilter in his life. He didn't want to stop the game Sophie played with him, but neither did he want to go out anywhere with her, when he knew what was—or more to the point, what *wasn't*—underneath that skirt.

Stopping her from buttoning up the prim but pretty shirt, he softly ran his hands down the cup line of the blue bra.

"We don't need to go right now, do we?" he challenged, "Surely I can show you how much I appreciate you dressing up for me?"

Not letting her answer him, he crushed her mouth in a hungry kiss. Flicking one nipple through the lacy cup, he felt power rush through him at her moan, as she arched further up into his body.

At her moan, Artemais could smell her sex growing damp. That heated, musky smell of desire he had come to know as hers alone. He inhaled the scent deep into his body. He would crave that scent like a drug for all of his days.

His cock hardened and lengthened, pressed uncomfortably against the fly of his jeans. If he didn't get out of the damn things soon he knew he would probably come in his pants like a schoolboy.

Keeping his lips and tongue pressed against Sophie, he frantically pulled at his jeans, pushing them down his legs to his ankles. Finally placing his hands back on her breasts, exactly where he wanted them to be, he pulled one breast from the bra cup. As he played with the breast and nipple, he pushed her gently down onto the bed. For a short moment, he stared down at her pointed, aroused nipple before taking it into his mouth.

Biting gently down on it, he wallowed in the combined scent of Sophie and her arousal. She grabbed his head roughly and pulled him closer, spreading her legs underneath him in obvious invitation.

"So, Oh Lord and Master," Artemais had to grin, the way Sophie said it made it sound so mocking, but so arousing at the same time, "are you simply going to tease me, or are you going to fuck me properly?"

Trying hard not to laugh, Artemais lifted his head from her luscious breast, and glared down at her. Pressing his groin into her, and pinning her lower body simply beneath his hips, he ground his iron-hard cock into her soft skin.

"You *are* a saucy thing, aren't you? Next time you call me your Lord and Master, you'd better use a little respect, girl."

Grinning at their play, he flipped the pleated skirt up to her waist, and nearly choked on his laughter.

She wore the skimpiest piece of lace he'd ever had the pleasure of seeing. The same royal blue as the skirt and bra, it couldn't possibly pass as a pair of panties. It looked like a pair of hipster panties, with a low-cut waist, yet the legs were cut scandalously high. It seemed to be literally two triangles of scanty lace barely held together. With her legs drawn wide, he could literally see everything, barely encased in blue lace.

Losing all his thoughts of teasing her and taking her inch-by-inch, so slowly she'd be begging for hours, he dipped his head to taste her sweet juices. Licking, then suckling her clit, he gloried in the fierce reaction Sophie had to him. As she arched into him, pressing down to get more pressure, all Artemais' good intentions flew out the window.

Rising, still with the taste and scent of her driving him nuts, he pushed his briefs down to tangle with his jeans, dropped back down on her, and thrust into her in one long stroke.

They both moaned at the filling pleasure. He felt so incredibly hard, he worried for a moment he might split her in two. When Sophie grabbed his ass and pulled him deeper into her, nails biting into him, he felt his control snap.

"Please don't tease me," she whimpered. "I need you right now."

Bending down to kiss her fiercely, he pumped himself into her, with long hard thrusts, flicking her clit to make her cry out. As she screamed her climax, he let himself go and exploded inside her, over and over.

Finally spent, he collapsed on top of her, breathing heavily.

After a few moments, having collected his wits, he smiled into her neck and enjoyed their combined scent.

"I never realized the full potential for crotchless underwear. I think I'm going to enjoy these panties."

Sophie laughed, holding him closer. He nuzzled her neck, enjoying the softer moment. Remembering his earlier jealousy, he spoke before he thought.

"Marry me, Soph."

She froze underneath him. Trying to think through the red haze of lust and possession clouding his brain, he tried to work through his confusion. When she boldly asked "Why?" his brain deserted him. Sitting up, he rubbed his head and nearly fell off the bed as his legs tangled with his jeans and created a large mess. What had been a moment of peacefulness became an awkward, confusing mess.

"What do you mean, why?" he stalled.

"I mean," Sophie replied calmly, pulling her skirt down and tugging on the silk shirt, "Why do you want to marry me?"

"Uh," he thought madly. "Because you're carrying my baby." At her raised eyebrow, he thought some more, "And because I go mad with jealousy every time I see other men, my brothers included, flirt with you."

Sophie shook her head.

"You know your brothers mean well. They flirt because that's the only way they know how to be friendly to a female. It means nothing and you know it. And I refuse to marry you simply because of the baby. We can work something out about her."

"Him," he corrected automatically.

Sophie sighed. "Whatever. You might want to think a little more about that proposal of yours, Artemais. My answer is no."

With that, she stood up, pulled on a pair of running shoes, which looked ridiculous with the sexy skirt and shirt, and left the room, slamming the door behind her. Artemais felt totally stunned for a moment, he simply sat on the bed, his jeans around his ankles, staring at the closed door. Hearing the truck coming up the driveway, he wriggled to get himself dressed again, and rushed out of the room.

Racing down the stairs, he came to the kitchen just in time to see Sophie walking towards the woods, and his brothers piling out of the truck.

"Sophie!" he called out, knowing she wouldn't turn around or acknowledge him. *Since when had women become so damn difficult?* he wondered.

Having all three of his brothers watching his embarrassment didn't help matters. He stormed back into the kitchen and put the kettle on.

"Do you need pointers, brother dear?" Dominic teased as he entered the kitchen and sat himself down. "Last time I saw you, the two of you exuded sex and couldn't wait to get to the bedroom. Or is that the problem? You took her somewhere else and she's pissed at your lack of sensitivity?"

"Shut up, Dom," he snapped, setting up the percolator.

"Maybe we ought to get him some of those self-help videos? You know, those kiddie ones for the high schools, you put A into B and you shake it all about," Samuel added his two cents.

"Shut the fuck up, Sam," he snapped, snarling.

"Well, we can't very well help you if you don't tell us why Sophie is pissed at you, Art," William said gently. "So spill, and we'll see what we can do.

Artemais looked up at his brothers, all of whom now sat quietly at the table looking back at him. He felt a warm rush of love for them. No matter what problems they'd had and troubles they'd found themselves in, they had always been able to rely on each other.

"I asked Sophie to marry me," he confessed.

"That's fantastic."

"Why is she pissed then? Women like that sort of thing."

Artemais gave Dom a hard look. As usual, William's comment snared his attention. Sometimes his younger brother was far too damn perceptive for his taste.

"What reason did you give her?"

Artemais felt his shoulders sag.

"I told her it was best for the baby and I felt tired of being jealous of her with other men."

Three outraged *"Whats!"* made him hunch his shoulders even more.

"Well," he pouted, "I couldn't think of anything else to say!"

When he looked up all three of his brothers looked like they wanted to go a round with him out behind the barn.

"Art, man, you can't tell them that sort of crap! You have to say you love them!"

Samuel snorted at Dominic's perception. "Yeah," he sneered, "but how many women have *you* told you loved?"

Dom gave him back a dirty glance. "*I* haven't proposed to any, so I haven't needed to yet."

William looked rather pleased with himself, and much more like the old Will Artemais knew and loved.

"Art, buddy, you better go after her or she'll skin your

balls off and hang them from the front gate. Get down on your knees and grovel. She might forgive you."

"But…" Art trailed off totally confused; he hadn't realized he loved her until just then. When had this happened? "But…I didn't know…didn't realize…"

Looking around the table at his brothers, they each looked comically surprised and astounded at his lack of personal knowledge.

"Oh shit," he cursed, the crushing knowledge of just how badly he had screwed up his proposal. "She's going to kill me."

When his brothers laughed and agreed, jeering and adding filthy comments on what else he could do to appease her, Artemais stood up.

Pointing to each one in turn, he said in his most serious Big Brother voice "If any of you *dare* to mention to Sophie that I needed help in this…!" When they laughed more, he simply held their gaze to show just how serious he felt. They all sobered up and promised.

Artemais ran from the kitchen, scenting Sophie and determined to make it up to her, any way he could.

Chapter Twenty-Three

Sophie sighed and looked around her. She usually had such a good sense of direction, but these woods seemed to always turn her around and around in circles. She had been looking for that special spot Artemais had taken her to yesterday. She had found the creek, but she must have been following it the wrong way. Ten minutes of walking and she could neither see the house, nor anything else, for that matter.

Sitting down where she was, she looked at the gorgeous clear water and frowned, finally letting her mind wander.

It had come as a truly terrifying shock to realize she loved Artemais. She had been blissfully unaware of her state until he had tried to talk her into a marriage of convenience.

She frowned again; this whole situation felt like Artemais' damn fault. If he hadn't proposed, then she wouldn't have realized until later that she loved him, and she could have stayed with him until he realized he loved her too.

Damned men, she groused, *always screwing up perfectly good relationships.*

Sophie heard twigs snap behind her, and she turned to see Artemais walking towards her. She frowned and turned back to the river.

"I'm not in the mood to talk to you Artemais. Don't

you need to get back to the village to yell at poor Roland?"

Sophie resisted the temptation to turn around when Artemais didn't reply, but simply stood behind her, obviously waiting. Hunching her shoulders, she fought the impulse to stand up and fight him.

As the seconds ticked by, each one dragging out longer and longer, Sophie gave in to temptation. Standing up fiercely and whirling around she planted her hands on her hips and glared at him.

"How *dare* you ask me to marry you simply for the baby's sake? Do you have any idea how many children grow up happy and healthy and well-loved with separated parents? I would *never* deny our child her father, but neither will I live in a home with a man who simply wants to keep me around so I won't run off with his child."

"Sophie, I—"

"And how *dare* you rationalize your actions by saying you're tired of feeling jealous?" she continued, not even pausing for breath and totally ignoring Artemais' interjection, "How the hell can you be feeling jealous? Your brothers wouldn't do a single ungentlemanly thing, even if I asked them to, out of respect for not only you and me, but because they love me like a sister, not a lover! You're just pouting because there's no such thing as jealousy without love, and you haven't uttered a word about love! Not one single word!"

Belatedly realizing just how much she had told Artemais, Sophie turned back around to stare down at the small creek. She couldn't tell if she felt upset, or really angry. She seemed to be both, which confused the hell out of her. How can you be angry and upset at the same time?

Angrily, she blinked away the tears that formed in her eyes.

Damned pregnancy hormones! Damn them to hell!

She shrugged her shoulders when she felt Artemais come up behind her to lay his warm hands on her. She wasn't interested in his sympathy or pity. Picturing the mess she must look, she could only imagine how he cringed at having to soothe the irrational, weepy pregnant female she had become without noticing.

It was just too bad. Maybe she should just move back into the city?

"The guys are going to hang shit on me. You should have seen their outrage when I told them the excuses I gave for marrying you."

"Excuses? I don't recall asking you to marry me. It's not needed in this day and age Artemais."

Sophie felt his sigh brush across her neck. She felt the gooseflesh rise, and the heat of his breath caressed the nape of her neck as he rested his head against her shoulder, pressing in.

"I know you don't *need* to marry me, Soph. But I really *want* to marry you."

Sophie bit her lip, refusing to ask "Why?" again. She didn't think her heart could take any more male rationalizations. When Artemais sighed and rubbed his face into her back, she knew she wouldn't like his next statement.

"The guys told me to tell you I loved you. And I swear it hit me right in the balls. I didn't realize I did until they said it. I don't think they'll ever respect me again. They were laughing their asses off when I ran from the kitchen. They'll never take advice from me again. But I swear it's true."

Sophie felt herself turned into Artemais' embrace. She didn't resist, she wasn't sure what sort of thoughts were running jumbled through her head. All she knew she felt was the first warm trickle of hope run through her blood.

Sophie looked up into Artemais' deep blue eyes, and saw love and honesty shining within them.

"I swear I do love you. I love the way you smile and tease me. I love the way your hips swing when you're tempting me. I get hot and hard when you simply look at me." Artemais placed one large hand over her still-flat stomach. "I want to go to the doctor's with you. I want to be there when we get our next ultrasound photo. I want to be there when our son is born."

"Daughter," Sophie mischievously injected.

"I'll make a deal with you," he replied, laughter glinting in his eyes. "You pick the girl's name, I'll pick the boy's name, and we won't let the doctors and nurses tell us the gender. It'll be lots of fun in the delivery room making you eat crow, and saying 'I told you so.' How about it?"

Sophie laughed. She quieted down when Artemais took both her hands in his and went down on one knee, right there in the middle of the forest, the damp earth seeping into his jeans and staining them.

"Sophie Melanie Briggs, will you do me the very great honor of becoming my wife and mate in all ways?"

Sophie stared down at Artemais. She smiled slowly, letting her love for him show through her own gray eyes. Pulling him upright she leaned into him and kiss him fiercely.

"I will. I love you too, Artemais, I didn't realize until I

was so very mad at you for those dumb-assed reasons for marriage. You can be the biggest moron sometimes."

She kissed him hungrily, pulling his shirt out of his jeans so she could run her hands over his warm chest. Feel his heart beat faster and faster as he became turned on and his magnificent cock rose to attention. She blinked, surprised when he pulled away slightly, regretfully.

"I'm so sorry darling. I need to go back to the village..." he trailed off, regret and frustration etched into his face.

Sophie smiled, knowing what she could do in the intervening hours.

"That's okay, I knew you had to go back. But I want you to promise to put off your brothers on tonight's poker rematch. Tell them we can do it tomorrow. I want to make plans for us tonight. Upstairs in your rooms."

Artemais smiled hugely, cock still straining against his jeans.

"I'll look forward to it. I'll leave William here with you." At Sophie's raised eyebrow, he hastened to explain, "I don't want you alone if your afternoon sickness is really bad. He can cook you something nice and bland for lunch that you hopefully won't bring back up again. I want to take Dominic and Samuel with me to see and speak to this Roland guy."

Sophie frowned, "Artemais, promise me you will listen to him. His mother ran off on him when he was just a boy, and he's had a hard life. Play nicely with him okay?"

Sophie couldn't read the expression he wore, but it seemed almost as if pieces of a puzzle were falling into place.

"I'll be taking him to see old Mona. I won't beat him to a bloody pulp, I promise."

Taking his hand in hers, Sophie started walking in the direction she assumed the house stood.

When Artemais cleared his throat, and oh-so-politely inquired in a bland voice, "Where are we going, love?" she smiled, trying to look worldly and innocent at the same time.

"Why I'm leading you back to the house, where else?"

Sophie laughed at Artemais' wry expression as he turned her ninety degrees and started walking in a totally different direction.

"I think I'll have to invest in a compass and map for you sweetheart."

Sophie laughed harder.

"I can't read a map, or use a compass. The arrow always points north. Now it's interesting to know which direction north is—but how the hell does that help me if I'm lost? You might want to know I also have trouble reading a map."

Artemais sighed the long-suffering sigh of a man in love.

Chapter Twenty-Four

Artemais knocked a little more loudly on the door to the small cottage.

"Hey Mona!" he called, "Can we come in, please?"

Artemais, Samuel, Dominic and Roland stood on the small front porch. Dominic had a large grin on his face and a sack full of groceries in his arms. He eyed Roland up and down, trying to disconcert him. Artemais leaned over and growled, "Be nice" into his ear. As he stood back, a tiny old lady opened the door. She seemed wrapped in a patchwork shawl and an ankle-length dark blue skirt.

"This had better be good," she mumbled, "you're interrupting my nap and Jerry Springer. Oh, it's you young Artemais." She stood back and opened the door wider. "What have you got there, little Dominic?" she eyed the big grocery bag distrustfully.

Dominic bent down and kissed her cheek.

"Some bread and milk and meat, Mona. And a container of your favorite Rocky Road." A small smile appeared on the old lady's face.

"Well, I might just put the kettle on then. Come on in you four."

Artemais felt much better when he realized Mona knew there were four of them. She often ignored someone until she had something to say to him. Hopefully she could answer a few questions he had. Manners were everything to Mona. He had warned Sophie and William they might be gone until dinner, as Mona would likely take her own sweet time telling them anything they wanted to know.

As he and Dominic helped Mona set up the kettle and tea, cups, and saucers, everyone was quiet. Roland and Samuel sat precariously perched on thin wooden chairs. Roland wasn't sure how Samuel felt, but he worried one wrong move or strong gust of wind would splinter the tiny chair. So he simply looked around, feeling perfectly happy to stay a while and see what would happen.

When all five of them sat comfortably around the small fire, tea and cookies in hand, Mona surprisingly came directly to the point.

"It's good to see you back, young man. I was worried after your ma died and your idiotic father took you away so we'd never see you again."

Roland choked on his tea. "Excuse me, ma'am?"

Mona looked at him, a tiny glint of laughter in her eyes.

"Don't you speak plain English? Which part didn't you understand? The part where I called your father an idiot, or the fact I called you a young man. Every man a day under seventy is young to me."

Roland blinked and set his teacup down on the small table nearby.

"My mother isn't dead, ma'am. She simply ran away from my father."

Mona shot a scornful look at him, then resumed eating her cookie.

"Don't be daft, boy. Your mother told you she'd come back for you, right?" Mona glared at him until he nodded. "Then what else could have kept her from coming back for you? She loved you dearly, she merely needed to warn the Pack of your father's evil intentions."

Artemais noticed that Roland went a few shades paler at Mona's words. He swallowed, but didn't contradict her words.

"So his mother had been one of the Pack," Artemais confirmed, leaning forwards.

"Oh yes," Mona smiled, taking another sip of tea. "She had her own problems, but she was dealing with them admirably once she married that man and young Roland here came along. Your daddy was sick, mentally sick. I couldn't tell exactly what illness it was, but it ate away at his mind—physically and emotionally. He had a lot of issues, that man, and when Janine finally got fed up with him and tried to help him deal with his hatred of himself, well, it became a bit messy, let's just say." She paused for just a moment.

"He swore he'd cleanse himself by ridding the world of the rest of the Pack. Janine tried to warn us. Young Roland here was barely three, so she thought he'd be safer at their home than with her in the park. Plus, she couldn't really take care of him while she changed, could she? So she came to warn us. We all started our moon time, but Jeffrey came and killed many of the Pack while we ran. By the time we realized the next day that Janine had left young Roland with his father and not someone in the village, Jeffrey had taken the boy away. I always thought he did it to avoid the sheriff's questions. Me and Sally— that was my sister—looked, but couldn't find them. We were too busy helping you and your brothers adjust to the great loss and taking care of your Grandfather. Another cookie?"

Artemais took the offered plate, nabbed a cookie and

passed it on to Dominic, then to Samuel.

"What happened to your father, Roland?"

"He died of syphilis when I was thirteen."

Artemais looked like he wanted to make a comment, but Mona was nodding, almost to herself and ignoring him.

"Ah yes. Syphilis. New name, old complaint. Well now, young Artemais, have I answered your questions?"

He smiled down at the elderly woman.

"Almost, Mona. Why didn't you mention to me years ago that there might have been another werewolf running around? I could have tracked him down and helped him."

"He had to come on his own. He hasn't known what he is—what his mother had been—and he has had his own private demons to fight. Right, young man?"

"Very true, ma'am."

Artemais would later swear that Mona blushed.

"Enough of the ma'am business. You can call me Mona, love. Your mother was like a daughter to me, and I watched over you enough when you were a baby. You'll be sticking around, won't you?"

Artemais watched as the young man and old woman forged a bond, and knew that everything would be fine. He and Dominic cooked up some of the steak and potatoes for Mona, while she reminisced about Roland's mother. When they were finished, Mona thanked them and walked them to her door.

"You stay with these nice young men until after the full moon, then you come back here when you're ready and we can talk some more. Right?"

"Yes, Mona. I won't be going off anywhere."

"Thank you for cooking my dinner, it's nice to see some men these days knowing how to use a kitchen for its proper purposes." This said with a glare and shake of the head to Dominic. Artemais briefly wondered if the old lady knew what Dominic's favorite purpose for a kitchen was. Seeing the glint in Mona's eye, he figured she did.

"I'll see you boys later. Stay safe."

With that she shut the door and they headed back to the Jeep. Artemais felt keen to get back home, back to Sophie, and see what her big plans for tonight were.

Chapter Twenty-Five

"Are you sure you're all right, Soph?" William asked again, concern furrowing his brow. Sophie sighed. She wished like hell William wasn't here, seeing her like this.

"I'm perfectly fine," she lied. She choked on the last syllable and leaned back over the toilet, dry retching. She hadn't anything left in her stomach for over five minutes now, but tell that to her nausea.

When it finally passed for another moment, she sat back down on the cool tiles and accepted the fresh washcloth William handed to her.

"Are you sure you're okay?" he asked again. Sophie gave up.

"William, my stomach is trying to kill me, or maybe simply turn itself inside out. I feel like I'm dying and will be fine in about half an hour. Most women get morning sickness, I seem to be cursed with afternoon sickness. So stop asking. Talk to me about something else."

William took a step back from the vehemence in her words. She felt a moment of guilt, which passed as soon as she saw her meaning had reached William.

"What do you want me to talk about?" he asked gently.

"Anything," she moaned, leaning back over the toilet, "Just don't make me think of how much I hate being pregnant at this point in time."

"Well, I don't really have anything much to say that

doesn't revolve around 'Are you all right?' and we've already covered that ground."

"Fine," Sophie snapped, "Why the hell are you so depressed half the time?"

The silence lengthened as Sophie's stomach tried vainly to wring out some more of whatever so mortally offended it. When the nausea finally passed again, she sat back down and took a few deep breaths. Looking back up to William, she stared at him.

"Well?"

William sighed in capitulation. He needed to talk to someone, and it looked like Sophie had designated herself as his confessor.

"I met this woman..." he trailed off. Sophie realized then and there this something lay heavily on his heart and getting the story out would be like pulling teeth. Thankfully, William continued.

"We dated for a while." *One month, two weeks and four days*, his brain injected, "and then she just upped and left with no warning and without saying goodbye last week."

Last Friday, sometime just after dawn while I lay sleeping after bringing her to orgasm five or six times, his brain chimed in, as it always did when he thought of Josephine. He squelched the familiar melancholy, preferring to be nonjudgmental so Sophie could give him her honest opinion on what he should do.

His pride and his heart had been tearing his brain to pieces over this problem since the second he had realized she had left him. He kept fluctuating between being angry over his pride being hurt at her casual leaving, and being worried sick that something might have happened to her.

He must have packed to follow her a million times in

the last week. He had finally simply kept a small suitcase packed under his bed. But every time he reached for it, determined to track his woman down, his wounded pride reared up, insisting he couldn't run after a woman like a lost little boy. The conflicting emotions were tearing him up. Maybe a woman's perspective would help here.

"I have no idea why she left or where she's gone. All I know is she was obviously more important to me than I was to her—otherwise she would never have left without a word. That really hurts and gets me a bit down."

Sophie crossed her legs under her, obviously thinking very deeply about his situation. He felt his load lighten as he shared it. Sophie was a great girl; smart and funny and Art really deserved her. He knew their bachelor lives would be different now, and a whole lot more interesting with Sophie around for the ride.

"I presume you were sleeping together?" Sophie managed to keep a straight face while she asked this. The thought of *any* of the Rutledge brothers having a platonic relationship made her want to have a fit of giggles. The women in the surrounding towns and villages probably knew all these guys intimately. While the thought of Artemais being intimate with any woman stung a little, the teasing potential for the other brothers was simply too good to pass up on.

"Well?" Sophie pressed, a huge grin on her face. William merely cleared his throat and blushed a little.

"I really don't want to comment on that Soph, you understand."

Sophie rolled her eyes and sighed.

"Fine! Well, I presume this girl—what's her name by the way?—wasn't simply moving houses, or changing jobs or something?"

William shook his head.

"Her name is Josephine, and I don't think she planned it at all. That's why my pride took such a beating Soph — I can't understand why she ran from me. She left her apartment with no notice, and broke her lease. She left her job with no notice. She was only waitressing, but she didn't even stop to collect her pay. I know I'm not an ogre, but surely she could have at least said goodbye before she left? Or explained what it was I did wrong?"

Sophie blinked, wondering why the hell William hadn't mentioned this before.

"William, I can only think of a few reasons why a woman would run like that. I am assuming here that she wasn't in an abusive relationship with you? You hadn't had some major argument about politics or religion or something, had you?"

"Of course not! Sophie! How could you possibly — "

"Yeah, yeah, just checking. Well, I don't know about you, but I can only think of two reasons a woman would leave everything behind, including her paycheck. Either someone is chasing her and she got scared, or she's pregnant. I can't see any woman running away from what pretty much consists of her life, simply to get away from you."

Sophie glared meaningfully at William. Letting her words sink in. He started to shake his head, then paused. Opened his mouth, and when no sound came out snapped it shut again.

Sophie looked carefully at him, wondering if he might have paled a few shades from his normal tanned complexion. When he started fiddling nervously with his long ponytail, she knew her words had started to take root.

"So. Was she running or hiding, or have you knocked her up and not followed through?"

William paused for another moment, obviously thinking furiously.

"I don't think she's pregnant. But I couldn't really say. Art has told us that only a true mate can be fertile to an Alpha. I'm second-in-charge, if — Heaven forbid — anything ever happened to Art, I'd take over until your child comes of age. So no, I don't think she is pregnant."

Sophie looked intently at William, waiting for him to continue.

"But…I am wondering…she was always so reticent about her past. Neither of us shared volumes of information and we'd only known each other about two months. But she always ducked the mandatory questions, and…sidetracked me. I just don't know…"

Sophie, feeling much better now, shuffled over and sat next to William, throwing an arm around his shoulders.

"Buck up, boyo. You can track her down, check that she's okay, and still be back in time for the birth of baby here. You *are* planning on tracking her down, aren't you?"

William nodded. "Yeah, I've been thinking about it since the day she left. It just never seemed to be the right time. But now that you're here, and baby is on his way, Art's line is secure and I'll have a bit more freedom. As long as I don't move out too far, I can call in the Deputies to cover for me and take some vacation time."

"I think that's a great idea, William. Now, what say we practice a little poker to spiff you up for tomorrow night's rematch?"

Grinning impishly as William groaned, Sophie took his arm and led him out of the huge bathroom and down into the kitchen.

"As long as we play for matchsticks," William bargained.

"How about for peanut butter and banana sandwiches? I'm *starving*. If I win, you make them, and if you win, I make them."

The look of disgusted horror on William's face had Sophie clutching her stomach with laughter.

Chapter Twenty-Six

It was nearly dark by the time Artemais, Samuel, and Dominic returned home. William stood in the kitchen, a steak and some vegetables sitting untouched in his spot on the table. When he saw Artemais come in he grimaced.

"You mate is revolting. She ate three peanut butter and banana sandwiches right here after her afternoon sickness. It nearly turned me off my own dinner. I had to open the windows and air the damn kitchen out. She teased me that this was all normal for her, that she *enjoys* eating carrot cake and chocolate topping! You have to do something about her, Art!"

Artemais grinned.

"That's okay, I'll go up and talk to her about it."

Ignoring the sniggering from William and mirth-filled stare from Dominic, Artemais headed up his private staircase into his section of the house. Already hard as a rock just thinking about what Sophie had planned for them, he opened his door and quietly closed it behind him.

Grinning hugely, he called out, "Honey! I'm home!" feeling a large, warm spot just over his heart.

The knowledge that he could come up here every day and every night and have Sophie here, ready and waiting for him... Artemais frowned a little as he reached his big bed. It was turned down, with a number of extra pillows and cushions thrown onto it, but he didn't see Sophie lying waiting on it. Many candles lay scattered around, on tabletops and windowsills, giving the room a soft, muted glow to it. His gas wall heaters were on, making the room comfortably warm.

"Sophie?" he called out, heading towards the bathroom. He figured he had merely arrived before she had finished getting ready.

Before he could knock and enter the bathroom, she came out from his study.

"Hey there. I thought it was you. You might want to get into something more comfortable. Like nothing but your robe," she said, nodding to the bed where she had laid out his silk robe. Artemais looked confused at the foam mats she carried and spread out on the bedroom floor.

"Uh, Soph, sweetie…"

"Come on. I'm in charge of tonight—so you'd better be able to follow orders."

Artemais didn't know whether to laugh or be very worried when he saw the impish gleam in her eyes. Deciding to play along for now, he began to strip. Wiggling his hips in the same manner he had seen strippers do back in his wilder days, he felt a blush creep up his cheeks when Sophie laughed and wolf-whistled.

A bit disappointedly, he realized Sophie had on her new purple camisole and a long purple-blue sarong style skirt that reached her ankles. Shrugging, he figured there hadn't been a skirt invented that he couldn't remove.

Pulling on his robe, he turned around, ready for whatever Sophie had planned next.

"Lie down on the mats, I'll just get the oil," Sophie waved to the mats she had spread out on the floor and hurried over to the dressing table and grabbed a bottle of what looked like massage oil.

Artemais sat down, intending to find out what was going on.

"Soph. What are you doing?"

"Pampering you. I'm going to give you the best damn massage you've ever had. I found this oil in the ladies' store, and I became inspired. Come on, don't be a killjoy. Lie back and I'll start with your feet. We can get rid of the robe soon enough."

"Hon, it isn't my feet that want a massage," he jeered, leaning over to kiss her on the cheek. She laughed and pushed him away.

"Oh, come on. Haven't you heard that anticipation makes it better? Just think, next time I'll let *you* be in charge if you're nice to me."

Nuzzling her neck now, he quickly licked the spot on her neck where his mark lay.

"I can be *very* nice to you love. Just let me show you."

Laughing, she pushed him down onto his stomach and shuffled down so she could pull his foot into her lap.

"I know your brand on *nice*, Mr. Rutledge, and I'd rather you saved it for late. Now just lie back there and let your mind wander. It's certainly not every day I'll be doing this for you. In fact, soon enough *you'll* be doing this nightly for *me*, if half the pregnancy stories I've heard are correct."

Artemais got himself comfortable, and closed his eyes. Sophie poured some of the oil on her hands, rubbing them together to warm them up, and began to massage his feet. He hadn't ever really paid any attention to his feet. But he now realized that there could be an awful lot of tension stored down there. As Sophie kneaded out knots and tensions that he hadn't known were present, he found himself moaning in relief at the strong but gentle manner her fingers worked.

"So what are your plans for tomorrow, darling?" she finally spoke.

"Mmmff," he grunted, not yet capable of speech. Finally, he replied, "I need to catch up on work tomorrow. I'll spend most the day in my office downstairs, catching up with business, and then I can show you around the woods. Hopefully point out a few landmarks so you won't keep on getting lost. *Ouch!*" As Sophie slapped his ass, he turned half around, twisting so he could see her grin down at him.

"That wasn't very nice. Just showing me landmarks would have been enough said! I'm not stupid, I know why you'd be showing them to me. So what sort of work do you do? You mentioned a security company?"

Artemais turned back around as she continued her massage.

"Yeah, my brothers and I own and run Rutledge Security. Or, it pretty much runs itself nowadays, but I like to keep up-to-date with it all, so it won't get out of hand."

"Rutledge Security? *The* Rutledge Security? Isn't that the biggest company and home security system? I didn't really connect that."

Artemais grunted again. "Samuel has done wonders for us with all his tinkering and gadgets, so he's branched out into a small private investigations firm. He's still loosely connected to the main company, does some cheaper work for us, but mostly he has his own clientele and business. Dominic plays with all the computer coding and solves the majority of our hacking problems. William decided to become the sheriff around here and play cop."

Artemais stopped talking as Sophie moved her way up his legs. He felt her moving over him, could smell her scent mingled with the lavender of the massage oil. He pressed his cock harder into the foam mat, hoping to give himself even a tiny measure of relief from the pressure building there. When Sophie took her hands away from him, he didn't know whether to howl in relief or despair.

"Let's get rid of this robe and move on to the bed, hmm? I think I have enough oil on my hands to do your back."

Standing up and stripping off the robe in one movement, Artemais stepped over to the bed and crashed down onto it. Lying on his back, hands behind his head, he grinned at her.

"Like I said before darling, it's not my back or feet that want a massage. If you're determined to ignore old Fred over here, you can massage my chest while straddling my hips. That might give me the strength to wait a few more minutes."

Sophie laughed at him.

"Old Fred? He never seems that old to me. But okay, I can massage your chest."

Artemais drew in a deep breath, praying for strength and patience as Sophie removed her sarong, revealing a scanty purple silk thong. As she straddled his hips, the damp heat of her core pressing down onto his rigid cock, he bit his lip to stop the groan that tried to escape.

As she rubbed her slick hands over him, the only thing Artemais' lust-filled brain could concentrate on was the wetness and warmth of her hands. How they must be a parody of how wet and warm her pussy must be. How it would grip him like a glove, like a vise and squeeze him for every drop of his seed.

Just as he *had* to tell Sophie to stop teasing him, to let him enter her, he felt her warm hands grasp his wrists. Thinking she would finally let him touch her, he didn't resist. Until he heard a metallic *snap* click into place around one wrist, and instantly the next.

"What the...? Sophie, what are you doing?"

Pulling on the fur-lined handcuffs, Artemais looked up at his love as she smiled.

"I wanted a bit of time to pamper you. I figured the easiest way to get you where I want you and not having you seduce me within seconds was to...er...restrict your movements. I also found these at the shop. It's really well-stocked, huh?"

Unbearably turned on, but also angry at the same time, Artemais pulled on the cuffs. If he didn't mind breaking his headboard, he could easily pull the cuffs through the broken wood, but Sophie looked so proud of herself he didn't want to ruin the moment for her.

Then his brain finally kicked into gear. If she had bought these from the local shop...running his thumb along the outside of the cuffs, he felt the remover catch. They were a gag item, and were specifically designed for easy removal. He supposed he should be grateful she hadn't stolen William's cuffs. Not only were his only unlockable by the single key only William held, but they had been custom-made so that even a werewolf had to struggle to break them.

Hmm...maybe he should let Sophie have her way, then turn the tables on her later.

Settling, making himself as comfortable as his randy

cock would allow, he raised and eyebrow, tauntingly.

"Okay then, wench. Do your worst—or best, depending on how you feel."

Sophie grinned. She leaned down and kissed him so thoroughly, so passionately, he felt his toes curl. As she kissed him, she stroked his nipples. When they peaked, and he involuntary arched up into her caress, she smiled and nibbled his lower lip.

"Bet you never realized a man's nipples are just as sensitive as a woman's."

Artemais tried to catch his breath.

"They aren't."

Sophie merely smiled.

"Sure they are. They're just sensitive in a different way. Watch."

Artemais felt all the blood rush from his head as he watched Sophie bend down over his chest, her short blonde curls no barrier to his eyes, and she took his nipple in her mouth. In his mind, he could see their positions reversed. He saw Sophie, bound and helpless before him, saw his own head bending down over her nipples, suckling them as she now suckled his. When she bit down gently on it, he cried out and arched himself into her.

"Oh shit, Sophie. Don't tease me. Take me now." Artemais held onto his control as she rolled her gray eyes up to him, watched him watch her as she suckled first one nipple, then the other.

The seconds ticked by, as Sophie watched him and he watched her. The moment was incredibly erotic, the picture she made, head bowed down, but eyes turned up to watch his reaction...he knew this picture would be etched in his brain for all his remaining days.

"So you want more, hmm?" she spoke around his nipple.

Mouth dry, Artemais could only nod his assent.

Sophie angled her head back down, and kissed her way down his chest, letting her hair drag silkily against his heated skin. She seemed to leave a trail of fire behind her, as the silky ends of her short hair caressed his skin and caught amongst his own lightly haired chest and abdomen.

When she continued downward, kissing and nibbling, her hair driving him wild, her scent enveloping him, he realized where she was leading him, he groaned and bucked his hips, hoping to hurry her up.

Before he reduced himself to begging her, he felt her hot, moist mouth close around his rigid cock. Moaning and thrusting his hips into her mouth, he rattled his cuffs, surprised to be reminded they were there. He desperately wished he could cup her sweet face, pull her further down onto his pulsing cock.

"Sophie," he panted, "please take me deeper. *Please.*"

As she chuckled, the vibrations drove him wild, making him even more desperate. He wanted to pleasure her, to have her come with him, but she seemed determined to do this her way tonight.

Just as he thought he had begun to control himself by biting down on his inner lip, Sophie started wetly pulling his balls into her mouth. She rolled them around, playing with them with her tongue, careful to keep her teeth out of the way. Feeling himself being driven over the edge, he cried out as his cock lengthened and hardened even more.

Certain he would be coming onto his stomach, cold and alone, when he felt his cock start to spurt, he felt the heated dampness of Sophie's mouth enclose over him again, sucking him dry.

His body racked by the orgasm blasting through him, Artemais felt his blood roar in his ears, closed his eyes against the shooting lights that ran through his head. He felt himself explode, over and over as he shot every last drop of his seed down her throat.

Finally lying back against the pillows and soft sheets, sweating, Artemais caught his breath. Feeling Sophie crawl up his body to lie on top of him, running her hand through his short hair, he felt the blood start to circulate again and the noise in his ears die down.

After a moment, he felt Sophie nuzzling his neck and shoulder again. Grinning indulgently, he rubbed his chin against the top of her head.

"That was fantastic, love. Thank you."

Sophie's chuckle penetrated his brain.

"That was just the appetizer. I have a few more things I want to do to you, and they're all going to take a damn sight longer. That was just to take the edge off."

Grinning hugely, Artemais felt Sophie take his momentarily still cock in her hand and stroked it until he returned to full attention. He long ago had noticed he didn't need a long time to recuperate sexually, but where Sophie was concerned, the word *insatiable* began to have real meaning.

Noticing her elevated breathing and dilated pupils, as she fondled and played with his cock, Artemais surreptitiously removed the cuffs. Wiggling his fingers, he realized the furred cuffs had kept his blood flow perfectly intact. Other than a tiny ache in his upper arm muscles from straining against the restricted posture while he came, the cuffs had worked perfectly. He made a mental note to complement Sally on her choice of adult toys.

Slowly and carefully, Artemais reached down to stroke Sophie's cheek in the same intimate, gentle manner she stroked his cock.

It took her a few seconds to realize his hands were supposed to be bound. He could tell the exact second her brain registered the fact that his hands were in fact unbound. Her eyes widened, she sat up, mouth open.

Quickly levering his body so he flipped her over, coming down on top of her, Artemais grinned.

"Hmm...what say we finish this a bit quicker than you were thinking, eh?"

"Hey!" Sophie complained indignantly, "that's not fair. How did you get out of them? I didn't hear them break!"

"There's a release catch on them, love. They're a gag item, not meant to be used seriously."

Artemais laughed as Sophie stuck her tongue out at him.

"Next time, I'll use William's cuffs," she promised.

Bending down, unable to resist kissing her a moment longer, Artemais wallowed in her taste and scent. He could smell himself on her, and it made his cock harden even more.

Fondling her, he found her soaking, and perfectly ready for him. Ripping her panties from her, he pressed two fingers deep inside her. He gloried in her sharp intake of breath, the way in which she arched into his intimate caress.

"Oh my. I don't think I want to wait anymore,

Artemais."

Pumping into her slowly, but steadily, Artemais brought her to the brink of climax, then removed his fingers carefully.

Gasping, face and body flushed, Sophie grabbed his arm, determinedly pulling him back to her.

"Don't!" she chocked out, "Please! Artemais…"

Not touching her, Artemais lent down and pressed his lips against hers. When she struggled to pull him closer, for his skin to contact her, he resisted.

"What do you want, Sophie?"

"You," she choked out, impatient.

"What about me? I'm right here, love."

"I want your cock, hot and deep and so far inside me that I can't tell where you end and I start. I want you pumping inside me, so I can feel every inch of you filling and completing me. Right *now*."

Turned on by her hot words, he thrust himself into her in one long stroke. Pressing himself into her, he joined them from hip to mouth. Pulling her hips higher up to meet his cock's demands, he thrust into her, over and over until she shattered and climaxed in his arms. Barely pausing to let her catch her breath, he continued his strokes, long and even, until she was writhing again in his embrace.

"Oh, Lord. Just come, Artemais! Please! You're killing me with this pleasure."

Unable to hold himself back any longer, as he felt the first contractions of her pussy squeeze his cock, he let himself go, and shot into her, two, then three times.

They both clung to each other, tightly. Spent,

Artemais collapsed next to her, reaching down to pull up the covers. Tangling his arms and legs around her, he pulled his Sophie as close to him as possible, considering she was still half dressed. "Tomorrow we can go back to the city and move your stuff in here. We can also start arranging the wedding, signing whatever needs to be done. Then we can inform the village. They can help out with whatever you need, Soph. Is that okay?"

She murmured sleepily. Artemais kissed her, and resolved to talk it out with her the following morning.

His mate wrapped safely and protectively in his arms, one hand lying on her stomach, protectively over his son, Artemais fell asleep.

Chapter Twenty-Seven
Friday Evening – The Full Moon.

Roland stood in the middle of the forest. Surrounded on all sides by the huge, centuries-old oak, elm and pine trees, he breathed in deeply a lung full of clean, pure air. Feeling pleasurably dwarfed by the trees, he tipped his head upwards to stare at the sky.

The midnight blue canopy stretched seemingly from here into eternity. The more Roland searched the sky, the deeper he could see. Tiny silver stars glinted like diamonds, scattered helter-skelter throughout the deep midnight blue of the sky.

It was beautiful. He would love to bring Helene out here. Maybe in a few weeks he could. Already he felt more at peace. With Helene and their son out here with him he would make a faster recovery. The time had finally come for them to bond together as a family.

Feeling a faint touch on his shoulder, he turned; surprised he had become so engrossed in something as common as the night sky and his own long-suppressed fantasies. Artemais stood behind him, his brothers and other members of his Pack from the Village around him.

"You ready?"

Nodding, Roland could feel the power in this moment. The truth of understanding himself, and maybe one day, his mother. He could almost feel her, her spirit close by, attached somehow to these woods. She seemed peaceful, at rest. It sidetracked him and made him feel better.

Roland felt a strange pulling of power, from over to the East. Turning, wondering what was happening, he saw the huge silvery moon rise up over the horizon. Slowly, almost teasingly, like the most beautiful of stripteases, bit-by-bit she exposed herself to him and the others gathered.

After what seemed like years, but probably only lasted a few minutes, the huge, rounded full moon hung just over the horizon, and Roland's gaze could not waver from her beauty.

The pale glow around her edges, the tiny crevices and dints in her pale face, every single thing about the moon suddenly captured his heart and his attention. He could feel the silvery power wash over him, heat his blood and snare his utmost attention.

The scents of the wood converged upon him, the scent of the damp earth, the woodsy scent of the trees, the animal/man smell of those people around him. One by one the scents bombarded him, and still he could not remove his eyes from the full moon.

He felt his skin shiver, a sensation unlike any he had ever experienced. The scents rushed upon him, and he felt the strongest urge to go explore them, to follow wherever they might lead him.

"I'll be right behind you Roland, so don't worry about anything. Just let it all flow."

The words Artemais said reminded him of the safety and security his mother had always offered him as a baby. She had always said she would watch over him, be with him. Funny how he had shut all those memories of her love and devotion to him out, he should have realized long ago that she would never have left him.

As he felt a huge charge of love for his mother wash over him, a total acceptance of her desires and choices, he felt a rippling across his skin and through his muscles. Looking down at his arms, everything seemed to happen at once.

A blinding pain broke through his every bone and muscle simultaneously. He cried out—not fully understanding what was going on—and then he fell to the ground.

It took him a moment for his brain to register the melding and shifting of bones and tissues. And then the scents of the forest were sharpened a thousand fold. Scents were richer, deeper. It was almost as if he could *see* the scents that permeated the world. The moon seemed to sing at him, call to him, beckon him to play, to explore, to hunt.

Roland threw back his head and howled, in joy and discovery. The other wolves and people still surrounding him followed suit, howling to the earth and the moon. Artemais—still in his man form—stood right beside him, and bent down onto one knee.

"Go for it, Roland. I'll change and follow you, keep a watch on you. This is your night."

While Roland pondered how he could be a wolf and still understand the human words, he stared as Artemais shimmered, much as he figured he had himself, and within the blink of the eye he moved from man to wolf.

The human part of Roland's brain registered, "*Wow, that was neat!*" but his animal instincts were fully in control.

He lifted his head, sniffed, and ran off after a scent of game he found.

Throughout the night, Roland explored, followed and tracked. It felt so similar to his dreams, but so much more intense! Everything lived, breathed, seemed to have a beat and pulse. He could see and sense things he had never thought of, never imagined.

And always in the background, like a radio playing music, was the ever humming, silvery, shimmery face of the moon. She presided over everything like a devoted mother, watching over her charges.

Roland barely took notice of Artemais tagging his steps. Every now and then, when he strayed too close to a home with a family inside, Artemais would jump in, nudging and snapping at his feet like a protective daddy, herding him away. But for the most part, Roland was given free rein to go where he pleased, do what he wished, hunt small game and wallow in the scents of the forest and the earth.

Hours later, Roland found himself back near the clearing where he had started. The moon hung low in the western sky, its humming muted now, still discernable, but definitely waning. Feeling a sadness that his freedom was coming to a close, Roland faced the setting moon and howled. He thanked the moon, the earth and the forest.

Artemais had padded over to what Roland assumed were his brothers. Standing alone on one edge of the woods, he joined his cry of thanks to the moon with many of the other wolves present.

Before he could wonder how he would change back, Roland noticed a silver movement just to the edge of his vision.

From the shadows of the woods a huge, silver wolf emerged. Large and old, he stood firm and proud. His blue eyes glinted in the predawn light. Catching sight of him, the old wolf came beside him.

Roland had the unnerving sensation of being sized up. It was as if the older wolf weighed and judged him for something. He stared back, unconcerned.

Throughout the evening he had felt the loving presence of his dead mother, but more importantly, he simply *knew* Helene had reached him, understood just how special and pivotal this night had been for him. No matter what, he knew he had taken the first baby steps towards truly accepting and understanding what he was.

Roland knew with the help of these people, and the love of his Helene, he could start a new life, together with Edward. Tonight was simply the beginning.

The confidence of the knowledge of Helene's love and acceptance helped him meet the eyes of this large wolf. The old wolf made a motion with his head, and nipped at Roland's feet. Looking back at Artemais, Roland knew the acceptance and almost reverence of the Pack towards this wolf meant no harm would come to him.

Willingly he followed the older wolf deep into the woods.

They meandered further and further into the woods. After a while, they came to a tiny, rundown cottage. The big old wolf paused outside, then sat on his haunches. Roland also sat waiting for he knew not what.

As the moon sank over the horizon, he felt the now familiar tingling that proceeded the rippling of his skin. Shivering in the cold, Roland looked down to his very human body, pale and glowing in the darkness. A bit bashful over his nakedness, he looked over to the naked old man sitting across the dirt from him.

The old man appeared totally unconcerned of his nudity. He motioned with his head for Roland to follow him into the cabin. Entering the surprisingly warm cabin, he donned the offered shirt and jeans.

"I got these from your Helene. She and your son will be arriving in a few days. We have a lot to talk about between now and then, but I think we both need some sleep first. I'm not as young as I once was. You're welcome to the main bed. I'll sleep on the futon out here."

Roland winced.

"No, really. I can sleep out here—"

"Don't be daft, boy. It won't make an ounce of difference to me. We can talk later in the day. Better be off, boy. I only need four hours sleep. You need more than that to recuperate."

Roland looked at the older man carefully. He really *looked* at him. He found absolutely nothing, with any of his senses, to make him concerned. Added to that he trusted Artemais. No way would he have helped him all this night and then let some fruitcake take him away. He could ask his questions later.

"Helene is okay?"

The old man nodded. "And your son is fine, too. Go to bed, boy."

Roland shrugged and headed off to the bedroom. Time enough for questions later.

Epilogue

"*Aaaaarggghhh!*" Sophie moaned, obviously in pain.

"That's wonderful, darling, just push *with* the contractions, not against them. Our son will only come when he's good and ready."

Sophie leveled a glance at Artemais that would have felled a lesser man.

"Our *daughter* can damned well be ready to come right now. I've had enough of this labor bullshit."

Suddenly, an obviously brand-new, top-of-the-range with every-gadget-included digital camera was stuck in her face.

"Come on, sis," Samuel crooned as if she were a frightened bird and not a heavily laboring grown woman, "Tell my little nephew that he's doing well. He might get a complex after having you calling him a girl for the last seven months."

Sophie growled at him and tried not to grin at her brother-in-law.

"Listen here, you goob. If you stick that camera in my face or any other orifice again, I will personally get up and stick it in one of *your* orifices that will make your life particularly unpleasant. Am I understood?"

She sighed when Samuel did nothing more than grin charmingly, toss a curl of his shoulder-length hair out of his eyes as it fell out of his short ponytail and wink at his other two brothers.

At least William and Dominic have the good sense to stand by the wall and not annoy me, she mused, crying out again as another contraction hit her hard. Artemais clutched her hand a little tighter and in his *I'm-being-gentle* voice suggested, "Maybe we should try some of those Lamaze breaths that you made me learn with you in that class, sweetheart?"

Sophie tried valiantly for a minute or so, but when another contraction hit her she gave up, preferring to try and break her husband's hand instead. That was far more satisfying.

"I'm going to kill you," she warned Artemais. "I am going to personally castrate each and every male on this planet. Those dicks of yours are lethal weapons and men ought to have a license to use them. *Aaargh!*"

Closing her eyes against the intense pain, Sophie missed the huge grins exchanged between the brothers.

"I see a head!" the doctor called out. Sophie had tried to be nice to the poor man, shadowed over by the four huge, burly men who were in his delivery room, but had forgotten him until he mentioned the head of her daughter.

"Pull it out!" she cried out impatiently, "Damned if I'm going to wait for you to list every one of her body parts!"

Artemais chuckled and positioned himself behind her, bracing his body against her back and holding both her hands.

"Now, come on sweetheart, you've come this far, surely you're not going to let *a man* birth our child?" he teased.

"Damned fine point," she conceded. And began to

push through the intensifying contractions. She felt too much pain, so she instead concentrated and focused all her energies on producing her little daughter. She couldn't be bothered with expending the breath to yell at Samuel hovering with his new camera, or William and Dominic hovering ready to catch their nephew in case the doctor missed.

Just before she felt that last push arrive, she had a flash. A nearly grown woman, who still seemed partly a girl, laughed and twirled before her in a brightly patterned summer dress. The girl's curly blonde hair was the image of her own. But when the girl stopped twirling to look at her, Sophie saw her bedroom blue eyes, the very image of her father's. The young woman blew her a kiss, then continued twirling and laughing in the sunshine. Sophie realized the girl danced in the grassy meadow out behind their big house.

"Christiana," she whispered, intuitively knowing her daughter's name.

"I think that's a lovely name," Artemais replied, assuming she spoke to him. Over the past few months, everyone in their family had put in their ten cents for the child's name. Artemais and his brothers had finally decided on Theodore for a boy after their father.

Over the last eight months not once had Sophie backed down on her decree this child would be a girl. Artemais and the boys had simply smiled indulgently. She intended to hold their disbelief of her intuition over their heads for years to come. And use it for all it was worth in the following years.

Finally, the last push came, and with a cry from both mother and daughter, the next generation of Alpha Rutledge wolves was born.

"It's a girl!" the poor doctor pronounced.

Sophie didn't even need to say anything. She merely smiled and tried to catch her breath. Looking at the stunned faces of her brothers, and the camera whirling on her little girl, Sophie grinned her pride. She could feel Artemais choking for breath behind her, his brain obviously fried from the long hours of the labor.

"Are you sure?" Artemais finally croaked out, obviously not believing the doctor competent.

"See for yourself," he replied happily, laying Sophie's now clean daughter on her stomach. Winking at Sophie, he crossed the room to start cleaning his utensils and probably breathing a sigh of relief his birthing room would soon be free of this family.

Sophie checked two sets of perfect fingers, with their tiny nails, two little baby feet and the obvious gender of her firstborn child.

With the tiny patch of blonde fluff on her head, and what Sophie knew would prove to be her father's blue eyes, Sophie felt a happiness and peacefulness she had never known well up in her.

Snuggling her baby close, Sophie decided not to tease with *I told you so's* and simply sat up, kissed her blissfully quiet daughter's head, and handed her over to her father.

"Artemais, this is Christiana."

Placing the newborn in his arms, she felt tears trickle down her face at Artemais' stunned expression.

"She's a girl."

Sophie rolled her eyes. Unable to hold back any longer, she let her amusement out.

"Well of course she is, what have I been telling you for

the last seven months?"

"But the tests were inconclusive, the doctors couldn't tell from the ultrasounds... Samuel said he saw his...there's never been a girl born to us..." Artemais stopped speaking when Christiana grabbed his nose and pulled.

Laughing, he stood up and walked over to his brothers.

"Look! I have a girl!"

Sophie rolled her eyes, secretly pleased at the doting, silly expressions her brothers-in-law held as they cooed, made faces and boastings of what *they* would teach Christiana. With three uncles that big, and an already obviously overprotective father, Sophie knew her daughter would be the safest and most protected young woman on the planet.

When the guys looked at each other, and turned towards her, Sophie wondered what they were doing. As they stepped up to the bed and all knelt, Artemais handed her back her daughter. Raising an eyebrow in query, she carefully took Christiana back and waited for the explanation.

"We want to know if Christiana Rose would be acceptable to you."

Rose had been their mother's name, and Sophie knew it would crush them if she didn't accept it. Smiling happily, with another damned tear rolling down her face, she nodded. Before she could speak, Christiana raised her fists, and started to cry for her dinner. "I think even Christiana agrees with her new name. But I also think she's as demanding as the rest of you. I'd better feed her and get some rest. I think I'll need it."

William, Dominic and Samuel all stooped to kiss Christiana and Sophie and then rushed out of the room, animatedly talking about pink frilly dresses and Barbie dolls. Sophie rolled her eyes and secretly hoped her daughter would become a tomboy—just to confound her uncles.

Sophie started Christiana suckling, then lay back on the uncomfortable bed. As she was wheeled into her little room by the orderlies, she had to smile at the protective and possessive way Artemais watched every move and step the poor men made.

Finally back in her own room, Sophie yawned, totally exhausted. She sat up, nodding her head to indicate Artemais should lie in behind her. As he made himself comfortable, and his arms crept around both her and her new little daughter, Sophie had never felt so safe or comfortable.

Wrapped protectively in her husband's arms, both Sophie and Christiana fell asleep.

HIDE AND SEEK:
RUTLEDGE WEREWOLVES

Elizabeth Lapthorne

Preview

**Coming soon in print to Ellora's Cave
Publishing, Inc.
Available now in eBook format at
www.ellorascave.com**

Josephine sat in the dingy bar and stared sadly down into her Lite Beer. She grimaced as she took a sip and wondered, not for the first time over the last three months, what the hell she was doing.

Avoiding that creepy, dingy boarding house you're staying in, came the mental reply.

Josephine sighed again and took another sip of the truly awful beer. Her realization was sad, but unfortunately true. She, Josephine Lomax, was most definitely avoiding the rat hole she currently called home. On her way back from her twelve-hour shift in a borderline seedy café where she had found a job as a waitress, she had decided to stop off at a slightly-less-seedy looking bar to relax, unwind from her hard day, and kill some time before she collapsed in bed from exhaustion.

So here she sat, surrounded by dirty, smelly men, sipping a beer she detested, all in the name of not going home.

Kind of depressing when one thought about it too clearly.

The shrill feedback from a microphone pulled her out of her spiraling depression and made her try to focus on the tiny stage through all the smoke. Squinting, she could barely make out in the half-light four, or maybe five, men setting up what appeared to be some instruments.

Smiling for the first time all week, Josephine settled back on her bar stool and relaxed. If there was to be music, maybe she could stay for an hour or more. She had sorely missed music, the thrum and beat of a great piece of soft rock or jazz. The quasi-classical crap most of the bars and cafés she worked in hung around the very bottom rung of the ladder of music, generally being very bad background music in the attempts to deter people ripping the place apart.

Even if the band only played half-decently, it would be a massive step up for her and cheer her up immensely. Finally she had found the perfect thing to get her going through the next week.

Josephine squinted and tried her best to catch a glimpse of the men setting up. They seemed to be the band members themselves, joking and laughing with each other under the din of the patrons. Josephine concentrated on them, soaking up anything exciting and different in her life.

Yet none of this seemed to explain the racing of her heart, the thudding excitement pumping in her blood. She brushed her thoughts aside, assuming anything new and exciting and screaming of *normal* would give her exactly the same reaction.

The great examples of eye candy she could view, even through the dim, smoky bar atmosphere had nothing to do with it, she assured herself.

A minute later, when the band seemed to have settled itself, a main spotlight, followed by a second one, shone on the men, illuminating them.

Josephine felt her breath catch. Had she thought half-decent eye candy? She must be going blind! The men were *gorgeous*. Looking about her, she wondered where the hysterical, screaming women were. Surely a band this sexy would have a dedicated fan base of teeny-bopping, skinny, blonde adoring women?

Yet the patrons had not changed, had barely moved as the opening of a well-known rock song began. Dirty, smelly men for the most part, tired, overworked waitresses, desperate for the tips and money they were making. Smoke curled from numerous cigarettes, and other things she didn't want to think about, as the patrons continued to drone on and play cards and pool, pretty much oblivious to the band.

It was as she watched the crowd in wonder at their sheer stupidity and lack of taste that she felt the eyes bore into her.

Turning around quickly, she looked once more at the band, *The Howlers*, as they were billed. The four men playing were all definitely handsome by any standard, maybe even truly deserving of the title drop-dead gorgeous, yet Josephine looked more closely at them.

The drummer seemed to be the leader of the group, calling the timing of the song and steadily searching the bar for…what she didn't know. Someone? Some threat? The saxophone player seemed slightly pissed. He winked at the waitress, raising his eyebrows suggestively. When one particularly young one blushed and nodded at him, he seemed to relax, his temper abated. The vocals man crooned his lyrics, eyeing yet another waitress and blowing a kiss to the one the sax man had already seemed to lay claim to.

It was as her eyes caught the bass guitarist she realized it was he who watched her. As she studied him, memorized his features, she realized the strong similarities between the men could only mean they were related. *Brothers?* She wondered.

The guitarist didn't stop looking at her, couldn't seem to take his eyes from her. She took her time looking him over, wanting to be able to identify him later if trouble should erupt.

Let's be honest with ourselves at least, she chided herself.

Fine. He's absolutely stunning, make-your-panties soaked, drop dead gorgeous and the best eye candy I've seen in months, since even before I left Seattle. Happy?

The silence in her head had her smiling slightly, the closest she'd come to smiling in a long, long time. The man truly was delectable. It was hard to tell with the drummer sitting down, but she felt certain he was taller than both the guitarist and the saxophone man, and only maybe an inch shorter than the vocals man. He seemed well over six feet, and lean in an athletic way.

Strong, and very sure of himself. He exuded a raw power, different from the drummer, who certainly now seemed to be the eldest and thus in charge, but the guitarist seemed to have his own brand of power. Not the seductive, wicked quality both the vocal and sax men held, but a quiet, rock-like strength.

The bass guitarist caught her staring. When her eyes clashed with his, he grinned hugely, the smile lightening his face and making him seem like some sort of playful god. Strong, self-assured, with a steady, rock-like quality to him. Josephine shook her head. Maybe the light beer tasted awful, but she couldn't possibly be tipsy from the few sips she had taken over the last half hour or so.

The man's smile was so infectious, so genuine, Josephine couldn't help herself, she smiled right back at him, her normal, cheery, devil-may-care grin that always made her feel cheeky and wicked. The man studied her further for a moment and then nodded his head, as if he had decided something. He winked at her and paid no attention when the vocals man slapped him on the shoulder in that manly, playful way brothers often have.

The time from then on seemed to pass in a happy, carefree blur. Josephine no longer cared that the bar stank, that the beer tasted repulsive or that the clientele was not exactly safe. She sat and watched the four men interact and jibe each other, singing to the crowd and entertaining themselves, if not some of the patrons.

During their first break, the tall bass guitarist headed towards her. His stride, confident and strong, made her quiver, whether in nerves or excitement she didn't know, and didn't particularly care, either.

He glared at the man next to her until he mumbled something rude and shifted to the next bar stool away from her.

The man sat down and grimaced at her beer.

"It's awful stuff, I know. I do not recommend it at all." She stopped, wanting to kick herself the second the words left her mouth. Surely he wouldn't be stupid enough to think she was warning him away or something? Before she could rush on and make a bigger fool of herself, her guitarist smiled and spoke to the bartender.

"A Coke for me and the lady will have…?"

Josephine smiled at him. "A white wine spritzer please."

The man nodded at the bartender, who shrugged and moved to get the drinks.

"I'm William Rutledge. What are you doing in such a dive?"

About the author:

Elizabeth Lapthorne is the eldest of four children. She grew up with lots of noise, fights and tale-telling. Her mother, a reporter and book reviewer, instilled in her a great appreciation of reading with the intrigues of a good plot.

Elizabeth studied Science at school, and whilst between jobs complained bitterly to a good friend about the lack of current literature to pass away the hours. While they both were looking up websites for new publishers, she stumbled onto Ellora's Cave. Jumping head-first into this doubly new site (both the first e-book site she had ever visited, as well as her first taste of Romantica) they both devoured over half of EC's Scent of Passions in less than a month. While waiting for more titles to be printed (as well as that ever-elusive science job) Elizabeth started dabbling again in her writing.

Elizabeth has always loved to read, it will always be her favourite pass-time, (she is constantly buying new books and bookshelves to fill), but she also loves going to the beach, sitting in the sun, having coffee (or better yet, CHOCOLATE and coffee) with her friends and generally enjoying life. She is extremely curious, which is why she studied science, and often tells "interesting" stories, loving a good laugh. She is a self-confessed email junkie, loving to read what other people on the EC board think and have to say, she laughs often at their tales and ideas. She recently has developed a taste for the gym. She's sure she read somewhere it was good for her, but she is reserving judgment to see how long it lasts.

Elizabeth welcomes mail from readers. You can write to her c/o Ellora's Cave Publishing at 1337 Commerce Drive, Suite 13, Stow OH 44224.

Also by Elizabeth Lapthorne:

Lion In Love
Payback
Rutledge Werewolves: *Hide and Seek*

Why an electronic book?

We live in the Information Age—an exciting time in the history of human civilization in which technology rules supreme and continues to progress in leaps and bounds every minute of every hour of every day. For a multitude of reasons, more and more avid literary fans are opting to purchase e-books instead of paperbacks. The question to those not yet initiated to the world of electronic reading is simply: *why?*

1. *Price.* An electronic title at Ellora's Cave Publishing runs anywhere from 40-75% less than the cover price of the <u>exact same title</u> in paperback format. Why? Cold mathematics. It is less expensive to publish an e-book than it is to publish a paperback, so the savings are passed along to the consumer.

2. *Space.* Running out of room to house your paperback books? That is one worry you will never have with electronic novels. For a low one-time cost, you can purchase a handheld computer designed specifically for e-reading purposes. Many e-readers are larger than the average handheld, giving you plenty of screen room. Better yet, hundreds of titles can be stored within your new library—a single microchip. (Please note that Ellora's Cave does not endorse any specific brands. You can check our website at www.ellorascave.com for customer

recommendations we make available to new consumers.)

3. *Mobility*. Because your new library now consists of only a microchip, your entire cache of books can be taken with you wherever you go.

4. *Personal preferences are accounted for.* Are the words you are currently reading too small? Too large? Too...**ANNOYING**? Paperback books cannot be modified according to personal preferences, but e-books can.

5. *Innovation*. The way you read a book is not the only advancement the Information Age has gifted the literary community with. There is also the factor of what you can read. Ellora's Cave Publishing will be introducing a new line of interactive titles that are available in e-book format only.

6. *Instant gratification.* Is it the middle of the night and all the bookstores are closed? Are you tired of waiting days—sometimes weeks—for online and offline bookstores to ship the novels you bought? Ellora's Cave Publishing sells instantaneous downloads 24 hours a day, 7 days a week, 365 days a year. Our e-book delivery system is 100% automated, meaning your order is filled as soon as you pay for it.

Those are a few of the top reasons why electronic novels are displacing paperbacks for many an avid reader. As always, Ellora's Cave Publishing welcomes your questions and comments. We invite you to email us at service@ellorascave.com or write to us directly at: 1337 Commerce Drive, Suite 13, Stow OH 44224.

Printed in the United States
28496LVS00007B/1-48